INVITATION TO A CRIME

H . BEDFORD-JONES

INVITATION
TO A CRIME
FURTHER ADVENTURES
OF DENIS BURKE

H. BEDFORD-JONES

ALTUS PRESS • 2016

© 2016 Altus Press • First Edition—2016

EDITED AND DESIGNED BY
Matthew Moring

PUBLISHING HISTORY
"Justice" originally appeared in the April 25, 1933 issue of *Short Stories* magazine (Vol. 143, No. 2). "Rendezvous" originally appeared in the May 10, 1933 issue of *Short Stories* magazine (Vol. 143, No. 3). "Rescue" originally appeared in the May 25, 1933 issue of *Short Stories* magazine (Vol. 143, No. 4).

THANKS TO
Everard P. Digges LaTouche, Joseph Laturnau and Gerd Pircher

TABLE OF CONTENTS

I

JUSTICE

An American Gentleman of Fortune
Makes His Bow in Morocco.

DENIS BURKE sipped his mint tea and listened to the two men who sat at the table with him, in the back room of the Meknez café. One was an Arab, bearded, arrogant. The other was a "colonist," as the French settlers were termed— a sallow, hook-nosed, voluble man whom Burke regarded without love.

"No," said Burke, wearying of the argument. "If I'd known your business with me, I'd not have met you here. I'll have none of it."

"But, m'sieu, it is much pay for little work!" exclaimed the Frenchman. "You are no angel; it is well known. You have run guns. You do many things. Here Selim has brought these letters. I take one packet; I deliver them to certain chiefs at Tadla and Ujda, and earn five thousand francs. You take the other packet to Rabat and deliver that—"

"No," said Burke, his blue eyes chilling.

"But why, in the name of the devil?" demanded the other. "Why refuse?"

"Two reasons," said Burke, lighting a cigaret and leaning back. He saw the door move slightly, but only shrugged. Too late now. "First, these letters of yours are really red propaganda, inciting the natives to revolt. I don't touch that sort of dirty stuff. And second—"

The door was flung open. Two men in uniform slid into the room, their pistols covering those at the table. In the doorway stood Captain Crepin, of the Intelligence, and his pistol was leveled at Burke.

"Well, M. Burke?" he demanded ironically. "Your second reason?"

Burke looked up. A slight smile touched his lips, his blue eyes danced, but he made no response. Crepin jerked his pistol.

"Stand up! All three of you—on your feet!"

Burke and the others rose in silence. Crepin swiftly searched the colonist, then the Arab. From each man he took small packets of letters. He came to Burke, frisked him, and a muttered oath escaped him. He flung a word at his men, who departed with Burke's two companions.

Then, closing the door after them, Crepin turned and regarded Burke, narrow-eyed.

"Once more you evade me, eh? You're smart, you are," he said crisply. Burke calmly resumed his chair and his cigaret.

"Right," he said whimsically. "Sorry I can't return the compliment, my dear Crepin. Thought you'd grab me with those two rascals, eh? And you really thought me capable of handling messy propaganda stuff! I'm disappointed in you, Crepin."

The clipped mustache of Crepin moved angrily.

"I can still take you along with them, you know—"

"Why don't you?" asked Burke with cheerful interest.

"Blast you! I've something better on hand for—" Crepin checked himself abruptly. "What was your second alleged reason?" he demanded.

"That I have other business on hand, naturally."

"Running guns, I suppose?"

"No, not until next month. Unfortunately, my business here is of a private nature, so I can't share it with you."

"You'll have time enough to share everything, ere long," snapped Crepin, then turned and stamped out of the room.

For three years Denis Burke had been in Morocco, and now things were rapidly coming to a head between him and Crepin. The intelligence officer blamed him, not without some reason, for a good share of the sub-surface turmoil of the country.

HAVING FINISHED his mint tea, Burke left a coin to pay for it, and quietly slipped out the back way. He came into a narrow, twisting street, far from the brightly lighted Rue Rouamzine. Certain that he was not followed, he knocked at a door. It was opened, and he stepped into a passage lighted only by a lantern.

"He is waiting, sidi," said the boy who had admitted him. "Come."

Burke followed, and was brought to a room where an old Arab lay on a brass bed, a black slave crouching beside it. At a word, the slave departed, and the boy brought Burke a stuffed leather seat. The wild eyes of the old man met his gaze.

"May Allah, the Compassionate, the Merciful, requite you for coming!"

"I rather fancy he will," said Burke, smiling. "It is about your son?"

"Yes. You can do anything. Have him acquitted! You are the friend of the helpless, and Allah knows I cannot move. Fifty thousand francs if you save him—"

"A life is a life," said Burke. "Why send for me? I am no lawyer."

"As Allah liveth, he did not kill the man!" exclaimed the Arab. "The case comes up before the pasha at Fez, day after tomorrow. That pasha is a millionaire; one cannot buy justice from him."

Burke repressed a smile. It was true. The pasha at Fez was a just man.

"Tell me exactly what happened," he said quietly. "The truth. All of it."

On its face, the story was simple. Ismail ibn Akbar had been to school in Paris, was an Arab of the new type, educated, intelligent, dissipated. His boon companions were certain officers of the garrison here in Meknez, a fast crowd. They frequented the villa of Count Rostoff—who, like many Russians of the old regime, had found a refuge in northern Africa. The countess was a remarkably beautiful woman.

Rustoff was found murdered, a crooked knife in his back. The knife belonged to Ismail. The countess swore that Ismail had been alone with Rustoff. So did two officers. Ismail's sole defence was that he had been drinking and remembered nothing.

"The officers?" demanded Burke.

"They were in another part of the house with the woman. Captain Blecourt of the Aviation, and Lieutenant Wiegand of the Spahis. All had been drinking. Here is the fifty thousand francs. I have more if you need it—"

Old Akbar clawed a packet of bank notes from beneath his pillow. Burke took it.

"If I can help him, very well. If not, I return the money. Now, about details—"

There were none. Akbar knew nothing else, had no clue whatever. With a shrug, Burke rose and took his leave. Friend of the helpless! Because Akbar had used those words, he would go on with the matter, hopeless though it appeared. Besides, Ismail had worked with him, and only last month had helped to put through that deal for rifles with the Azemour chiefs.

Denis Burke halted suddenly, and a whistle escaped his lips. So this was what Crepin had meant! Ismail might talk to save his own neck!

"Faith, there's more to it!" he reflected sharply. "That Rostoff woman is a bad egg. She's working with the intelligence corps—hm! This murder took place a week ago. If Ismail did it, they'd settle him. But they're not certain! They've offered him his life if he'll squeal on me, eh? Crepin believes he'll talk. Of course Rostoff wasn't murdered with this in view, but they took advantage of circumstances and nailed Ismail."

HE THOUGHT rapidly, as he came back into the Rue Rouamzine, then hailed a rental automobile that was honking its way toward the gate.

"The French city," he told the chauffeur. "41, Rue d'Aguedal, by the Cathedral."

It was still early; he would find Lourmel at home. Lourmel was the manager of a branch bank in the French city, and had dealings with all the garrison officers, chiefly of a money-lending nature.

The car plunged down into the ravine and took the long climb up the opposite slope to the hill on which stood the extensive French city. Burke leaned forward, eyes alert, watching the glittering lights above. He was on the trail now, inexorably running down the menacing peril. At those last words from Crepin, he had known that something was up, and now to unearth the secret!

Lourmel would talk. Like many another Frenchman in Morocco, he hated the military caste bitterly. Besides, Burke had worked with him more than once.

Twenty minutes later, he was seated in the library of a small villa. Lourmel, a thin dark man, listened calmly to his abrupt questions.

"Certainly, *mon ami*, I know Blecourt very well. He is an ox. Stupid, powerful, ever in debt or drunk; his family has money. In the air, a marvel. On the ground, a fool. The other, Lieutenant Wiegand, is different. Intelligent, alert, five times decorated for reckless bravery, three times demoted for affairs of wine or women, twice tried and acquitted for crimes of violence."

"The devil! You know a lot about these officers," said Burke.

The other grinned. "That is my business. If you have an affair with those two, dismiss Blecourt, but beware of Wiegand. He's a gentleman, a scoundrel, and always has money."

"Thanks. Do you know the Countess Rostoff?"

The banker threw up his hands. "No! Name of heaven, no! The count was a rascal; she got men into trouble, he blackmailed them. Keep away from her, I warn you! I know nothing against her; she has a spotless reputation; she has the devil's own beauty. Look out for that sort of a woman!"

"Mon ami, you interest me strangely," said Burke, smiling a little. "Come! There's a man's life at stake. So Wiegand always has money?"

"But not enough. He frequently needs more. The very day of Rostoff's death, Wiegand got twenty thousand francs from me. His note, you understand, was fair security. Besides, he could repay in three months. He is to be married to a banker's daughter in Lyons; the dowry is a large one. Oh, he's good for the money! But the odd thing is that he came in next day and repaid that loan."

Burke's eyes narrowed. "So? Gambling?"

"No; the same notes I had given him, apparently." Lourmel shrugged. "I don't ask questions, me. You're not mixed up with that woman?"

"I've never laid eyes on her," said Burke, and chuckled. "Don't ask questions, eh?"

"Well, with you it is another matter, one of friendship."

"Thank you," said Burke, and rose. "By the way, would it be possible for you to arrange a meeting between me and this Blecourt? Perhaps at luncheon tomorrow? I must go to Fez in the afternoon."

"Of a certainty. The Café de Paris, at one."

WHEN DENIS BURKE so desired, he could be the most charming of men. What with his Legion of Honor, his varied experiences, his individual outlook on life, he could also be intensely interesting.

Blecourt, a rather dull fellow whose whole existence flattened out at less than five hundred feet altitude, sat entranced for an hour or more, gulped down cognacs in rapid succession, and under Burke's deft handling confided his inmost fears. He was returning to France on leave in a month's time, and regarded the journey with actual horror.

"The *courrier* to Marseilles," he groaned, "and then the journey to Lyons. Good God, what horrible slow motion to anticipate! By air? But no, they will not permit it. And if I am to be best man at the wedding of my comrade, I must go, I must do my duty—"

And this was absolutely all that Denis Burke got out of Blecourt. The wedding of Wiegand was to take place on the fifteenth of the next month. They were going back on leave, the two of them, and Blecourt was already shuddering at the journey.

Oddly enough, however, this gave Denis Burke an idea.

II

THAT AFTERNOON, late, Burke drove over to Fez.

Once there, he left his car in the French city, and made his way to the little French hotel in Fez Jedid, or "New" Fez, so-called from being a scant thousand years old. Fez "Bali," or "Old" Fez, antedated it by a good hundred years.

Once settled at the hotel, Burke sought the bazaars of the brass merchants in the Rue du Tala. He entered one of these bazaars, which was owned by a cousin of Ismail ibn Akbar, and was presently seated alone in the rear room with the hawk-faced owner.

"It is not wise for me to try and see Ismail," he said abruptly. "Will you, therefore, take a message to him tonight without fail?"

The other assented. "Without fail, sidi, as Allah liveth."

"Good. Tell him these words: 'Promise to tell everything when you are brought before the pasha. If you do not see me there, tell. If you see me there, tell nothing.' Do you understand? Repeat the message."

The other repeated it gravely. Burke, satisfied, departed.

AT EIGHT that evening, Denis Burke pulled the bell at the gate of the Countess Rostoffs residence.

This was an old house in Fez Jedid. The street was narrow, overhung, broken by great massive doors and gates bearing the scars of many centuries. The gate of the Rostoff house was set in a massive wall, the building solidly adjoining those on either side. A lantern bearing an electric globe overhung the gate.

An Arab servant admitted Burke without question. Madame was at home, yes.

Across a little courtyard, down a colonnade, into an ancient dwelling that was a miniature jewel with its glorious woodwork, its carved and painted plaster, its tiles and Berber rugs. True, the rugs slipped easily on the tiles, but one looked out for this by instinct, as a rule.

Burke was standing in the reception room, sunk three steps below the surrounding level, when she appeared—slim, tall, very black hair and very white skin, her dark eyes cool and level, challenging yet perfectly poised. She put out her hand to him, unsmiling.

"M. Denis Burke! I have heard of you. It is a happiness to meet you."

Burke felt the subtle appeal of her, sensed the outpouring of her radiant personality enveloping him, steeled himself to evade her swiftly flung but invisible net. They were seated on the thick, high-piled pillows, with a low table before them.

Leaning forward, Burke laid a sealed envelope on the table.

"Madame," he said, when she had accepted a cigaret, and he saw her eyes seek that envelope with silent curiosity. "I have come to make an appeal to you."

"Indeed! How fascinating!" she replied gravely, smoking with a stately enjoyment. "You are seeking aid for some pet charity, perhaps?"

"Precisely. Who really killed your husband?"

She studied him for a long moment with lifted, lazy brows and casual interest. Denis Burke perceived that the shot had failed, that any shot would fail. This woman was impervious. She was an artist. She was an actress. An actress—ah! That was it.

"Really, I do not get your meaning, M. Burke," she responded at length, calmly. "What right have you to ask such questions?"

Burke regarded her with his whimsical, warm smile.

"The answer lies in that envelope; but let it be for the moment. Will you meet me halfway, frankly?"

She looked surprised. "But of course! You mystify me. Why would I not? Certainly I have nothing to conceal."

Burke sighed. "Faith, I'd like to wring your pretty neck!" he said, and there was no smile in his eyes as he said it. "Upon my word, I rather believe that you killed him yourself! I know all about the little games you and he played with other men. Yes, it's possible. Well, my interest lies in saving that Arab, Ismail ibn Akhbar. You know who I am, as you admit. Therefore you know that I might threaten you. But that would gain nothing."

"Nothing," she repeated, and feigned to stifle a yawn. But her gaze slipped for an instant to the envelope on the table. "Threats would not interest me in the least."

"Have you no human emotions?" said Burke savagely. She looked at him, and a slow smile came into her face, the first he had seen there. Under its radiance she was transformed, her beauty was heightened a thousandfold.

"Ah! Now I like you better," she said softly. And abruptly,

her whole manner changed. She flung off her grave and stately air, suddenly became animated, eager, intimate. "Yes, I'll tell you the truth, M. Burke. I can readily believe that you'd know a good deal about me, about us; you are in a position to know such things."

"As Captain Crepin probably informed you," said Burke. She shrugged at the thrust, and a low, amused laugh came to her lips.

"Crepin? Why discuss him? Well, it is true that my husband and I did not get on well, except as business partners. You see, I am really a business woman."

"So I have discovered," said Burke, regaining his cheerful mien. "In this envelope are fifty thousand francs. A high price for a man's life, in this country."

"Not nearly high enough for a woman's happiness," she said cryptically. Burke made a gesture of irritation.

"Enough of this fencing! You were in this house with three visitors. I don't believe that Ismail committed the crime, madame. There remain two others and yourself—"

"Monsieur, these other two men are gentlemen," she said quietly, calmly, cutting him short with an air of finality. "They are above suspicion. I can vouch for them in every way. As a matter of fact," she added, her eyes steady upon his, "I am about to marry one of them—Lieutenant Wiegand. Just as soon as it can be done, in view of the present circumstances. We have loved each other for some time, you comprehend. I tell you this in confidence, to make you realize that your errand here is quite vain."

Burke inclined his head silently. Truth lay in her words and her eyes. Against this woman he was utterly helpless. In defense of her love, of the whole structure of her future life, this woman who was a perfect actress would become a tigress as well. To preserve that structure, she would let one man or a hundred men die.

WIEGAND! EVERYTHING was clear now. An affair between Wiegand and herself; Rostoff the blackmailer; Wiegand desperately trying to hush the man, then killing him. And all the while there was the banker's daughter in Lyons— did she know of this? Well, it would be useless to tell her.

"Thank you. I understand. We will not speak of the matter again." Burke looked up. "Since we are momentarily on intimate terms, will you tell me whether Captain Crepin is a friend of yours?"

The quick flash in her eye made answer, even before her words.

"He is an enemy, with whom I have made terms."

Burke came to his feet and held out his hand.

"Madame, you have been very generous with your confidences. I appreciate it."

"Almost, M. Burke, you make me sorry that I cannot help you," she said, looking him in the eyes with a swift smile. "But I cannot. By the way, do not forget your envelope yonder."

Burke turned, but he did not touch the envelope.

Without a ring, without being even announced, a man suddenly appeared in the doorway and then stopped short, staring at them in astonishment. A lieutenant of Spahis.

"Oh!" The woman swung about swiftly, with a low, glad cry. "You! M. Burke, let me present Lieutenant Wiegand. You have, perhaps, heard of each other?"

Burke bowed. That dark, lean, vulpine countenance showed him instantly the type of man with whom he dealt.

"I am enchanted!" he exclaimed, as he met Wiegand's eyes with a laugh. "Monsieur, only this morning I was speaking of you, hearing of you from a dear friend who admires you intensely. I trust that I may offer my congratulations?"

Wiegand started slightly.

"I do not understand," he said harshly. Imperious passion showed in his face; a man of furious impulses, of terrific emotions.

"Why, your marriage on the fifteenth of next month!" exclaimed Burke gaily. "The banker's daughter in Lyons! Captain Blecourt was telling me of your plans to leave here together— poor devil, how he dreads the trip by boat and rail! He's to be best man, eh? The lady's name—what was it? Oh yes! Sylvie Bontrailles. Allow me to wish you every happiness, upon my word!"

The face of Wiegand was like a thundercloud split by terrible lightning flashes. Countess Rostoff stared at him, then bit her lip as though checking back impulsive words. A slight pallor showed in her features, a glitter leaped in her eyes.

Then Wiegand collected himself, and bowed slightly.

"I fear, monsieur, that there is some awkward mistake," he said coolly.

"Nonsense! Not a bit of it!" and Burke laughed out. "Eh? Perhaps I shouldn't have mentioned it, though? Oh, I say! I'm frightfully sorry—"

Wiegand drew himself up, then turned to the woman.

"My dear, will you have the goodness to leave us alone for a moment?"

"With pleasure," she answered coolly. "M. Burke, I wish to continue our very interesting conversation. When Lieutenant Wiegand has departed, I shall expect you in the next room."

Burke bowed silently.

WITH A calm look at Wiegand, she turned to the table, picked up the envelope that lay there, and with a casual air crossed the room and disappeared. Burke's pulses leaped. Then he found Wiegand before him, and fury convulsed the dark features.

"This was no accident, M. Burke," he said with a snarl in his voice, a frightful hatred in his eyes. "I have heard of you. I know what a scoundrel you are. I don't know what you mean by it, what you're doing here—but, by God, you'll regret that you came!"

Burke produced a cigaret and tapped it reflectively.

"That is entirely possible," he said calmly, and met Wiegand's gaze with eyes that were like blue ice. "By the way, it was very curious about that twenty thousand francs you borrowed, on the day Rostoff died—eh? And still more curious that it should have been repaid the next day—the very next day! Eh?"

It is a characteristic of swarthy folk that in moments of intense agitation, their color is intensified rather than lightened. Another man might have turned livid. Wiegand's features darkened and darkened as he met Burke's eyes.

Then he turned abruptly on his heel and strode out of the place.

Twenty minutes later, Burke was shown out by the Arab servant. The light burned over the sunken gateway; the street outside was narrow, dark, lit only at long distances by electric bulbs, and deserted as the streets of Fez are always deserted at this hour.

Burke, humming a gay air, started up the street.

As he passed a deep doorway a figure moved, stirred, leaped upon him. A shot rang out with fearful reverberation from the house-walls around. Burke staggered forward, half fell, then turned and grappled with his assailant.

After a moment, a second shot split the night.

III

ON THE following morning, the narrow, tortuous streets of Fez Jedid were no longer empty, but crammed with folk—Arabs, Jews, soldiers, men on donkeys, calmly plodding camels bearing merchandise. Pandemonium of voices filled the air.

Through this throng and tumult, Denis Burke walked from his hotel on his way to the court of the pasha; a purely Oriental court, near the Bou Jlou gate. As he strode along, he was acutely conscious of the powder-stains on his cheek, of the jagged cut over his left eye, and of the fact that he was being followed.

When he came into the Rue du Tala, he caught a glimpse of his shadower. The one had become two. Both were in mufti. They were Crepin's men.

Burke knew then that everything must have been discovered; but he went on.

Presently he reached the huge courtyard inside the gate, where a throng was now congregated. To his left was a doorless arch that opened into the long, narrow court room. It was not yet quite ten o'clock, the hour of court.

Now the two men openly closed in behind him. From the archway stepped Captain Crepin. Burke halted, and the intelligence officer stepped up to him with a curt nod.

"Good day, M. Burke."

"The top of the morning to you, my dear Crepin," said Burke cheerfully. "We seem destined to meet in unexpected places, eh?"

"You're under arrest," snapped the other.

Burke's brows lifted. "Important if true, captain dear. And may I ask why?"

"For the murder of Lieutenant Wiegand last night."

Burke met the flinty eyes with his whimsical smile.

"Murder?"

"Exactly. You bear the marks of the encounter, I see. Wiegand was found dying, shot through the body. He named you before he died. Upon the pistol that killed him were found fingerprints. They will be established as yours, as soon as we obtain your prints—"

"Oh, they were mine, certainly! I admit it freely," said Burke carelessly.

The other was astonished, stared hard at him. The two men had moved up, stood close on either side of Burke.

"Then you admit the murder?" rasped Crepin.

"By no means! Wiegand attacked me, I defended myself. He shot at me and I grappled with him. In the struggle, he was shot with his own weapon."

"A likely story. You have evidence?"

"Only my word."

Crepin stepped close to him. "M. Burke, I warned you the other night. This is the finish. I have a car close by. We'd better go into the French city and get the *proces verbal* done with, eh?"

"Wait," said Burke. "I'm interested in this trial of Ismail ibn Akbar."

"Indeed?" Crepin eyed him with grim amusement. "More interested than you know, I think. My advice is not to be present. Ismail has promised to tell everything, and will do so. However, I've enough on you now, Burke."

"None the less, I'd like to be present at the hearing," rejoined Burke with a shrug. "You know me, Crepin. I give you my parole, my word of honor not to resist or escape."

Crepin met his eyes, then reached forward and frisked him, finding no weapon.

"Very well. Come along."

Crepin's men remained outside.

BURKE AND Crepin walked up the long room. At the upper end a native clerk was writing busily. Beside the empty desk of the pasha sat the French commissioner, nominally an advisor, in reality the dictator of French policy. He nodded to Crepin, who fell into low-voiced talk with him. Burke took one of the wicker stools and settled down comfortably.

A moment later, with upraised voices and a stir of sound, the pasha entered. He was a thick-set, bearded Arab in pure white robes. He greeted Burke in surprised recognition, and went on to his desk, where he, too, fell into unheard talk with Crepin.

In at the lower end of the room came a man, who flung himself on his face, kissed the earthen floor, and began some impassioned plea to the pasha. The latter, irritated, made a gesture. Two brawny bailiffs threw out the plaintiff, literally. Silence ensued, save for the mutter of voices. Then the pasha straightened up and flung an order at the bailiffs by the entrance.

Between two guards, Ismail ibn Akbar was led in, dirty, disheveled, handcuffed. He knelt, bowed his face to the ground, and remained motionless. Crepin addressed him curtly.

"Ismail ibn Akbar! Stand up."

The man obeyed.

Crepin motioned to Burke. "Look at this man. You know him, do you not?"

Ismail's wild eyes went to Burke. He lifted his manacled hands.

"By Allah and Allah!" broke out his voice. "By the beard of my father, by the holy Al Koran, by the honor of the Prophet— I have never seen him before in my life!"

Burke's lips twitched. A red tide of passion flooded into the face of Captain Crepin; his clipped mustache quivered with anger. But before he could speak, Countess Rostoff entered the long room.

She was cloaked in the deepest mourning, but her heavy veil was flung back to show the lovely oval of her features. She ignored Ismail, Burke, Crepin. Her gaze was fastened on the French commissioner, and she addressed him rapidly as he rose and bowed.

"M. Desfarges, I desire to change my testimony in this matter. I will now tell everything—the whole truth! My husband was not killed by this Arab, who was dead drunk at the time. He was murdered by Lieutenant Wiegand."

A silence of amazement, of utter consternation, settled upon the room. The pasha, now suddenly become a mere nonentity, stared at the woman with kindling eyes. Captain Crepin, thunderstruck, moved as though to speak and then checked himself. The commissioner eyed her sharply.

"Madame, this is irregular. You have sworn—"

"I have lied," she broke in. "I appeal to the justice of the pasha!"

"By Allah, let her be heard!" exclaimed the pasha impulsively. "Why not?"

The commissioner nervously rustled his papers, glanced at Crepin, and shrugged.

"You admit perjury, madame?"

"I could not help myself! He made me do it!" Tragedy leaped in her face, filled her voice, as she burst forth in a flood of impassioned speech. "My husband was a man of the highest, noblest character! Lieutenant Wiegand pressed his attentions on me. He hated my husband, owed him money. That night he and Captain Blecourt had come, and this Arab with them. There was drinking. Lieutenant Wiegand went into the library with my husband. There was a struggle, followed by shouts. Wiegand killed him with this native's knife. Blecourt was half drunk, unable to realize—"

She paused, her bosom rising and falling, her voice choked. Burke eyed her with admiration. Then she rallied, before anyone could interrupt.

"Wiegand threatened me. Even at such a moment, he spoke of marriage—marriage!" The horror in her voice, in her face, held them all transfixed. "He had me in his power. He had previously compromised me; he had letters from me, which he carried with him always. They were letters written in momentary weakness—oh, I conceal nothing! He ordered me to say that Ismail had attacked and killed my poor husband. He impressed this story on Blecourt. The fool believed it, believed he had witnessed it!"

Her voice echoed through the room like the tones of a bronze bell. Even Crepin's wonted cynicism was shaken by the unfolding of this tragic drama. He stood staring, as though stupefied by what he heard. Suddenly the commissioner started.

"Eh, madame! Are you aware that Lieutenant Wiegand was murdered last night?"

"I know, I know—ah, *mon Dieu!* But he was not murdered."
A sudden sob shook the woman, then she controlled it. "Last
night M. Burke came to my house. He believed this Arab to
be innocent and pleaded with me for the truth. He is an honest
man, this M. Burke! Lieutenant Wiegand arrived unexpect-
edly, and became furious. M. Burke charged him to his face
with having accused Ismail falsely, and threatened to expose
his intrigues with—with another woman. Wiegand departed,
uttering threats. Shortly afterward, M. Burke left. I watched
him go, from a window. He had scarcely taken three steps when
a figure leaped upon him. There was a shot, a scuffle, and presently came another shot. Some time later, after the police
arrived, my servants told me that Lieutenant Wiegand had
been found dying.

"M. Desfarges, I must tell the truth now. I am free to do so.
The blood of an innocent man cannot rest upon me."

CREPIN STEPPED forward, and intervened harshly.

"If your story is true, then we are to believe that Wiegand
killed your husband? On your own bare testimony? After you
admit perjury?"

The woman turned to him with stately dignity.

"No, monsieur. Two of my servants saw my husband killed,
were unable to save him. They are outside now, unwilling wit-
nesses; I forced them to come and tell the truth."

Crepin blinked. "Eh! But these letters you mention—"

Burke rose to his feet.

"They are here," he said, and extended two letters. "I took
them from Wiegand's pocket last night."

Crepin took the letters. He glanced at them, then looked at
Burke.

"You expect me to believe that after a death struggle with
Wiegand, you took these letters from his pocket before you
escaped?"

"Certainly," said Burke calmly. "Why not?"

Crepin swallowed hard. Then the voice of the pasha, speaking as though to himself, lifted upon the room.

"The ways of God are inscrutable! By the Prophet, here is justice made manifest!"

Then he began to speak softly, rapidly, eagerly, with the commissioner, who could only nod assent. Captain Crepin stepped up to Burke, looked into his eyes, and spoke under his breath.

"Ah, you rascal! So once again you have the effrontery to cheat me."

Burke's blue eyes danced merrily, as he produced his cigarette case.

"Justice, my dear Crepin, is a magnificent thing! May I offer a cigarette?"

I I

RENDEZVOUS

*As the French Agent said to the Young American,
"Burke, you are a Scoundrel, a Rascal—
and I have a Certain Respect for You."*

BURKE WAS collecting his bets on the fourth race. It was a cleanup, an enormous cleanup. All around swarmed the money-mad throng—Arabs, civilians, soldiers, women. His hands filled with bundles of thousand-franc notes, Burke turned.

He collided sharply with Captain Crepin, who was of course in mufti.

A simultaneous word of apology broke from the two men. Burke's lean, incisive features broke into a whimsical smile as he met the eyes of the Intelligence officer. Crepin did not return the smile. His thin, mustached, severe countenance was menacing.

"A word with you, M. Burke," he said.

"Faith, my dear Crepin, I'm at your service!" returned Burke gaily, stuffing the sheaves of notes into his pockets. "You're always full of the most charming surprises!"

The other grunted sardonically, as they worked a way through the crowd.

The sun hung in the west, glittering on the snowy peaks of the Atlas that rise above Marrakesh. Nearby showed the new French city, lively, naked, spick-and-span. Off to the right, amid its glorious date-palm groves, lifted the savage red walls of old Marrakesh.

"I congratulate you," said Crepin acidly, "on picking the right horse."

Burke chuckled. "Congratulate me, rather, on having the right friends, my dear fellow! If you didn't make such a nuisance of yourself, I might let you in on something good tomorrow."

Crepin merely sniffed. Presently they were clear of the throng, and Crepin halted. He lit a cigaret and handed Burke one, surveying the trim, hard figure with the red ribbon of the Legion of Honor at its lapel. Burke held a match to both cigarets.

"M. Burke, I have a certain respect for you," said Crepin bluntly. "You're a rascal. A scoundrel. You've run guns to dissident chiefs. I intend to land you in jail or have you expelled from Morocco. None the less, you have a certain sense of honor which I appreciate."

Denis Burke bowed, and his blue eyes danced gaily.

"I may return the compliment," he said whimsically. "You're a bitter hard devil. You are devoted to your duty. You've no more human feeling than a snake, apparently. At the same time, you're a gentleman. Your mere word on any subject would be good with me."

Crepin inclined his head. "Thank you. In that case, M. Burke, I give you my word that I know your business here in Marrakesh. I know whom you expect to meet, what you expect to do. You've run your last gun, and your number is up. I advise you to leave here, leave Morocco, immediately."

Burke's brows lifted. "I like Morocco," he answered. "It likes me. I've been here for three years—"

"Raising hell."

"Making trouble, if you like. Well, expell me if you can! You've tried hard enough to get something on me. You've failed. You're too much of a gentleman to frame me."

"This time," said Crepin stiffly, "there will be no failure. *Au revoir!*"

HE STRODE away. Burke directed his steps toward the French town, at first in sober thought. His lips twisted in a grimace.

"A devilish unpleasant fellow, that!" he reflected. "Does he really know, indeed? Has somebody babbled that I'm here to meet El Hanech? In that case—but no, it's impossible! El Hanech sent me word to meet him at a certain time and place. His brother carried the message, was caught and killed an hour afterward. No one else could have spoken. Yet Crepin seemed damned sure of himself! Well, I'll chance it."

He swung along with his lithe, clean stride, nodding to acquaintances, exchanging occasional cheery greetings with cloaked Arab figures. He had cast his lot here in Morocco, and loved the country.

A certain part of Morocco, however, did not love Denis Burke.

Presently he was seated before a table, on the shaded terrace of a café. Across the railroad tracks on the far side of the square, was a glorious outspread view of Marrakesh and the palm groves. From this thronged square radiated all life and activity between the huge native city on the one side, and the enormous semi-circle of the French town, aviation camp and forts on the other side.

A short, bearded Arab, nearly black in complexion but wearing beautiful snowy garments, passed among the tables, saluted Burke, and pulled out the chair beside him.

"Peace be upon you, sidi," he grunted.

"And upon you, Si' Dris," said Burke in Arabic, then broke into a laugh. "How the devil you worked it, I don't know! But Fanchon romped home and paid twenty to one. I got your money and mine down. I've a bale of notes here—"

"Keep them until later; bring them to my office in the morning," said Sidi Idris, and crooked a finger at the nearest waiter. He accepted a cigaret from Burke, and smiled faintly beneath his white hood. "Not so bad for the first day of your visit in our charming city, eh? But there is better to come, by Allah! We have not seen you here for two months. There is work to do."

"You and I work together all right, Si' Dris," said Burke. "We can trust each other, and that's more than I can say for most! What kind of work?"

The Arab did not reply until the waiter had brought his mint tea and departed. He sipped the tea, his eyes stabbing about the place, then spoke softly.

"I have four boxes, small enough to be inconspicuous in the rear end of an automobile. Three of ammunition, one containing automatic rifles taken apart. We split thirty thousand francs for their delivery. A day's run from here."

Burke's eyes lighted up, then narrowed.

"To whom?"

"El Mekhnezi; he'll meet you on the highway near Jeb el Saghro."

"No," snapped Burke, and his gaze hardened. "That fellow's a blackguard, an outright murderer. He and his gang are lice on the face of the earth! To supply a fellow of that sort with automatic rifles would be criminal."

"Does it matter?" asked Sidi Idris gently. "You have taken guns to others—"

"That was different, and you know it," cut in Burke, his eyes glinting dangerously. "With El Mekhnezi, no! I'll help the right sort, but not the wrong sort at any price!"

"Allah i samah!" murmured Sidi Idris, and so dismissed the matter with the proverbial "God will pardon!" which his people apply to anything and everything. Presently he finished his tea and pushed back his chair.

"You are leaving?"

"Not yet, my friend," said Burke. "I have an appointment."

The other nodded comprehension, and took his departure.

DENIS BURKE lit a fresh cigaret, sipped his drink, and let his thoughts drift back to Captain Crepin. He had no hesitation in risking French anger, for he had potent friends among French, Arabs and Berbers also. Now that military rule was superseded by civil government, Crepin must step softly.

True, Burke lived by his wits, was an adventurer. He risked his neck by running guns with the same gay laughter that accompanied a big haul on a fixed horse race; but he sold his help to those who needed it. There was plenty of oppression in Morocco. The native chiefs, the great caids and pashas, were supported by the French; the feudal system still prevailed; slavery, even, was still in existence.

El Hanech was a typical case. That chieftain of a little Berber hill tribe was a doomed man. The French wanted to hang him, the powerful pasha who had taken his lands wanted to shoot him—chiefly because he had resisted oppression. El Hanech, "the serpent," could command money enough, but was too fiercely proud, too independent, too dangerous, not to be doomed. And Burke had come here to meet this man.

Precisely to the minute of the appointment made two weeks earlier, El Hanech came.

Burke had expected to see the man he knew, a wild blond savage from the hills, bearded, clad in arrogant Berber garments of filth and tatters. He was astonished to see a slim figure with a pure white *sulmah* flung over European clothes. Under the white hood showed a clean-shaven, hard-jawed face as white as his own, blue eyes as reckless as his own, a thin-lipped smile tinged with bitterness.

"Greeting, my friend!" said El Hanech in French. "So you would not recognize me, eh? Excellent. Neither will anyone else."

"You're a fool to come here," said Burke. The other took the opposite chair and threw back the white hood to display red hair. A strong man, vigorous, virile.

"No; it is safe enough. My shaven face is unknown. Well, the pasha has taken the last of my lands, all my cattle and sheep. It is the end. The French support him."

"And you dare to come to Marrakesh?"

"This is only the French city. No, I'm not going into the pasha's den yonder!" and El Hanech flung a glance over his shoulder toward the ancient city—of hatred.

"You are my one hope," went on El Hanech softly, looking back to Burke. "Behind the pasha are the French; to resist, were utter folly. If you had not kept this appointment, I would have gone into the city, sought out the pasha, and put my knife into his liver. My people have scattered with their possessions, among other tribes. For me there is no refuge. The pasha has put a price upon my head."

"And it's a damned shame," said Burke hotly. "Your family?"

"You have it. Three wives, two sons; no more. Six of us. As you know, my cousin Moussa lives in Larache, in the Spanish zone to the north, far beyond the power of this dog of a pasha. He is wealthy, a great man, with much land. He offers me an asylum."

"But how the devil will you get there?" exclaimed Burke,

astonished. "By train, you'd be pinched in no time, even if you had forged papers. You can't cross the frontier—"

El Hanech grinned.

"The frontier is nothing; Moussa will arrange that. You will arrange all else."

"Oh, will I?"

"Assuredly. Three days ago I killed the pasha's steward and took the year's taxes he had collected. Here is twenty thousand francs," and into Burke's hands he passed a fat roll of notes. "Get me an automobile. Have it at a certain place tomorrow night. Yes?"

BURKE POCKETED the money.

"Yes. Where?"

"On the Casablanca road. Once through the palm groves, you know the bridge across the Tinsift river? Just beyond is a fork, one highway branching off to Safi. At that fork, I'll be waiting. I'll send back the car from the frontier. Agreed?"

"Agreed," said Burke. "At eight tomorrow night."

"May Allah recompense you!" For an instant the Berber's hard face softened. Then he drew up his hood. "One thing more. My family lie out in the hills, a few miles away. They are starving. I will take back some food today, but we will need more, both food and water. Put some in the car. We have no luggage except rifles, so there'll be room enough."

"Very well," said Burke. "Do you think that Captain Crepin has any word of this?"

"Crepin?" The white teeth of El Hanech showed in a snarl that was like a wolf's snap. "That dog? No. Only I knew and my brother, who is now dead. And you."

"Then perhaps he guessed, for he gave me a warning." Burke shrugged and laughed. "No matter! I'll bring the car. Eight tomorrow night; be ready for anything."

II

BY NINE o'clock that evening, Denis Burke found that he was unable to rent a car in Marrakesh. December had come, the tourist season was on full blast, and every available car was out. The few other private cars he might have obtained were only diminutive Citroens.

Burke was not worried, however. The huge Transatlantique system of hotels, spread over the whole of northern Africa, was at his service. In the morning he could go to the "Transat" and get anything from a sedan to an autobus at five minutes' notice. So, with a shrug, he returned to his pension in the French city.

With morning, he passed by the office of Sidi Idris—who was a lawyer, with up-to-date offices in the French town—and left the other's share of the racing spoils. Then he went his way toward the savage red Marrakesh whose legions had poured forth to the conquest of Spain.

Coming in by the Dukala gate, he had only a few steps to go before reaching the charming old palace that had been transformed into the Transat hotel. Burke passed the gaily clad group of native guides clustered inside the entrance, and strode on to the desk, with a cheery nod to the French manager.

"Good morning, M. Dufresne! How are you off for automobiles this morning?"

"Ah, M. Burke! How goes it? Automobiles? Mon Dieu! I never knew such a season! It is terrible!"

"Good! I'll have no trouble getting a closed car, then?"

Dufresne spread his hands wide. "You misunderstand! The *courrier* that reached Casablanca yesterday morning from Marseille, flooded us with tourists. Trippers, season visitors, artists, Americans—name of a dog! It is terrific, it is formidable! Every company car from here to Fez has been engaged; every private car we could rent has been taken."

"The devil!" exclaimed Burke. "Look here, Dufresne. You

have a Fiat sedan yourself. Rent it to me for three days and I'll pay any price you ask."

The other looked sorrowful.

"Monsieur, I am desolated. But five minutes ago it, too, was engaged."

"By whom?" snapped Burke. Dufresne pointed across at the writing room.

"By that species of a camel in there. An Englishwoman— what a woman! One who walks like a man, and writes a book on politics."

"Her name?"

"Madame Stillwater."

Burke turned and strode across the glorious lobby, whose thick Berber rugs and old cut plaster decorations formed a riot of color. In the little writing room sat a woman of perhaps fifty, severely clad. At Burke's bow, she lifted frigid eyes.

"My card, Mrs. Stillwater; permit me," said Burke. For once that charming smile of his had no effect.

"I am not aware that I have your acquaintance, sir," said the woman brusquely.

"Faith, you are now!" and Burke laughed. Then he sobered. "Madame, I am in the most urgent need of a car for a couple of days. It is, I assure you, a matter of life and death. I find that you've hired the last car to be obtained in Marrakesh, that of the hotel manager."

"Certainly I have," she broke in coldly, without glancing at his card. "If you mean to ask that I let you use it, you're wasting your time and mine. I need that automobile myself."

"Not as badly as I do, perhaps," said Burke. "I'll be glad to pay the rent on it, and to offer you a bonus of five thousand francs."

SHE SURVEYED him suspiciously.

"No! It's for no good, I'll be bound. An American, by your accent; well, I don't intend to give up my comfort for American dollars."

"Ten thousand francs, madame."

Her brows lifted. "That is all. Good day to you."

"Twenty thousand francs, madame! I tell you it's a matter of—"

"And suppose I asked fifty thousand francs?" she demanded.

"Fifty thousand? Very well. I'll pay it—"

"You are certainly a madman," said the lady. "Will you kindly cease to annoy me, or must I have you put out?"

Livid with anger, Burke bowed and withdrew in silence. In this austere, frigid woman was utter finality—an absolute refusal to listen or comprehend.

He was appalled by what he had learned, a few hours too late. No time now to telephone for a car from Casablanca. He had no way of reaching El Hanech, who was lying out on some sun-scorched hillside. Desperate, he returned to the desk.

"Dufresne, I must have a car by five this evening. I'll pay twenty thousand francs if you can hire one for me."

Dufresne turned pale. "Twenty thousand! For that I would sell you the Fiat! But no, m'sieu. To rent a car at any price is impossible today. I have just had a telephone call from the Rabat hotel. A rich tourist there has offered any price for a car. It cannot be found. Automobiles, alas, do not grow on trees in Morocco! By tomorrow, it will be different."

"By tomorrow," muttered Burke, as he left the hotel, "the man who depends upon me will be lost."

Behind him, as the doors closed, a trim figure crossed the lobby, spoke briefly with the manager. The latter then accompanied him to the writing room and introduced him to Madame Stillwater. At her invitation, Captain Crepin sat down and spoke fluently.

"My dear sir," said the lady firmly, "I have whole-hearted respect for government. I knew from the very start that this man was a scoundrel!"

"You were right," assented Captain Crepin, fingering the card Burke had left. "He supplies ammunition and guns to dissident chiefs. He lends help to escaping prisoners. He laughs at the government, defies the Sultan himself."

"And you do not punish him?" exclaimed the indignant lady.

"First he must be caught. And this time, madame, I expect to catch him—with your help. Will you give it?"

"I shall, most certainly!" and flinty eyes were bent upon the intelligence officer.

Captain Crepin leaned forward and spoke rapidly.

DENIS BURKE, meantime, was walking along the dusty road toward the French city. He needed to walk, needed to think. A car capable of taking El Hanech and his family at top speed to the frontier—well, it did not grow on Moroccan palms, as Dufresne had said. A taxicab would be useless; one might get El Hanech as far as Casablanca, but there was too much risk. The Berbers must reach the frontier before daybreak, to be safe.

Sidi Idris? He would not help willingly. Arab and Berber regard each other with the virulent hatred of a thousand years. He would probably betray the Serpent. Burke could trust Sidi Idris with his life, but not with the life of a Berber chief.

"El Hanech has put his life in my hand, and I can't fail him," thought Burke desperately. "I'll get a car somewhere if I have to steal it—"

Ahead of him opened out the French city, with its bustle and thronging crowd filling the Square of the 7th September. Then Burke paused. He heard his name called, and turned.

"Sidi! Sidi Burke!" It was one of the guides from the hotel, stripped of his gay outer garments, running hard to overtake him. "A message! *Ya Lalla!*"

"Eh?" exclaimed Burke. "What lady?"

"She who is like a camel, sidi. She sent me for you, asks that you return."

Twenty minutes later, Burke once more bowed to Madame Stillwater.

"Mr. Burke, if that is your name," she said stiffly, "I have reconsidered. My first impression was that you were a very impudent young man, and I resented it. Perhaps I was wrong; not that I am often mistaken in my judgments, however. If you desire the car for three days, it is yours. I will accept no payment whatever."

Denis Burke could not believe his ears. With a sudden access of joy, he extended his hand to the lady, his eyes shining with delight.

"Madame, you are an angel!" he exclaimed warmly. "Upon my word, an angel! I thank you with all my heart."

"Never mind all that, if you please. The car is at your service now. I have spoken to the manager. Good day to you."

Burke withdrew, and scarce knew what was going on around him until he deposited the Fiat before the door of his own pension. Then he dared believe that it was true.

"The rest is simple," he reflected happily. "Gas and oil. Provisions and water. I'll have them packed in boxes for the sake of neatness and to save room. This car can go like the devil, and El Hanech can drive like another devil. Good! Tomorrow night he'll have the car back here. Couldn't be better!"

Burke had entirely forgotten that, on the previous day, he had refused to earn thirty thousand francs by delivering four small boxes to the bandit, El Mekhnezi.

III

AT SEVEN-THIRTY that evening, Denis Burke was switching on the lights of the Fiat, when a voice came to him in the darkness.

"Sidi! I am from Si 'Dris."

He was aware of a dark figure beside the car. A messenger, then.

"Yes?" he said. "What does Sidi Idris want?"

"A warning, sidi," came the response. "You have been followed, watched. Even now two misbegotten Arabs of the intelligence service are standing at the corner."

"Let them stand!" and Burke laughed a little.

"More, sidi. Captain Crepin has given orders, assembling his
men at seven-thirty."

Burke started. "Where? Quickly, in the name of Allah!"

"At the camp, sidi—"

Like a flash, Burke started the car, threw in the gears, and
went roaring away without lights. A faint yell drifted after him
from the corner. He was around another corner on two wheels,
shifted into second, switched on his lights, and swung into the
Avenue du Gueliz with the speed of a madman.

This wide boulevard went straight past the railroad station
to the great camp. But Burke was not headed for the camp.

Crepin gathering his men at seven-thirty—it was seven-
thirty now! Then it was a matter of minutes, as Burke realized
instantly. Ahead of him was a triangle. At the railroad tracks,
the Casablanca highway turned sharply right. Straight ahead
was the camp under the Gueliz forts. To block the highway,
Crepin must come from the camp; while Burke had only to
swing into it here ahead—

He sent the Fiat roaring along the street. Those watchers
must telephone to Crepin, who would then make a dash to cut
off evasion at the railroad bridge, just this side the rendezvous.
It was a gamble, a good gamble!

"Faith, I can make it—I must make it!" thought Burke,
leaning over the wheel. There was the railroad ahead. His horn
blared at a party of soldiers; they scattered with wild curses.
The car swung, the brakes ground, the tires screamed. The
Casablanca highway!

Crepin knew everything, then. The warning had been honest.
Somewhere, somewhere, there had been a leak. No matter!
Burke opened the throttle wide.

Up there at the fork of the roads was the hillman who trusted him, who depended absolutely upon him, with terrible simplicity. To El Hanech, this car meant life, safety for himself and his family. Without it, he was doomed.

And Crepin knew everything! The words rang in Burke's brain like a knell. Here was a rendezvous he must not fail!

What it meant to him, he knew well enough. He had intended to turn over the car and walk back to town; a few miles meant nothing. Now there would be no escape, no evasion. El Hanech would get away in the Fiat. Denis Burke must remain afoot, delay the pursuers, hold them ignorant of which road El Hanech had taken, there at the fork.

THERE WAS no way out, no choice. Burke crouched over the wheel as the car roared madly on, and cursed under his breath. He had given his word, and this was something Denis Burke had never broken. Prison—deportation—no matter! Another man had trusted him, and must not trust in vain.

The buildings, the outspread palm groves, were behind him now. An open stretch ahead, then the hills, the railroad bridge, the road-fork. The mileage needle quivered and mounted, but Burke never looked at it. Somewhere ahead, the road from the camp came into the highway. Crepin was beaten! Not a car in sight!

Burke felt the heart upleap in him, felt the wild surge of exultation that comes from victory. A laugh on his lips, he drove at the curving road ahead, found the low hills closing in. His insane speed slackened. No car could take these curves at such wild pace—

A sudden fierce oath burst from him. Around a curve now; and dead ahead showed two cars, their headlights trained on the road, figures of men strung out. The two were placed with converging headlights—barely space for a car to pass between them. A soldier stood there, waving a flag, halting him.

Burke did not halt. He knew instantly that somehow he had been outguessed. Crepin might have sent that messenger, in fact; the whole thing was a trap. A trap! The blood thrummed at his temples. The soldier was waving frantically now. There was Crepin, in the full headlight glare, waving a pistol. Other men with rifles.

"To hell with you!" roared Burke, and opened the throttle wide again.

Wild, shrill yells from either hand. The man with the flag leaped frantically for safety as the Fiat thundered at him. Burke crouched low, saw one of the two cars shoved forward. The fools! Trying to wreck him! A red spat of rifles.

Then a crash, a shuddering shock. The Fiat seemed to stagger, and next instant was roaring on again full speed. A bullet came through the rear window, smashed the windshield before Burke's eyes. He was through them, through! Ahead, his lights picked up the railroad bridge. Through them!

Then the Fiat plunged wildly.

Burke wrenched at the wheel with savage strength. Another plunge. A horrible lurch sideways, as the brakes screamed. Halfway down the descent, the Fiat swung across the road and came to a stop, with a tire shot out.

AND AHEAD, not half a mile distant, El Hanech waited.

A great sob broke from Denis Burke—half oath, half groan. Suddenly weak, he lowered his head on his hands, as they clutched the wheel. They were coming behind him, one car loaded down with men. No escape now, no evasion. He was taken. He had failed.

"Good evening, M. Burke," said Captain Crepin stiffly. "Will you descend, if you please?"

Burke obeyed.

"Devil and all!" exclaimed Burke, with the shadow of his old gay smile. "I gave you a run for it, anyhow!"

Crepin, standing beside him, shrugged lightly.

"You will have a long repose," he made dry response. "Out with those boxes, men! Smash into them."

"Why waste time?" said Burke. "You have me, you know."

Crepin smiled thinly beneath his clipped mustache.

"I have you, yes. But, my friend, I must have the evidence also."

For one wild instant, Burke stared. Had Crepin stooped so low? Was there some planted evidence in his car? Impossible! There was a crash of wood, another. Then startled faces were turned to the two who stood there, and sudden silence fell. A sergeant, prying into one of the smashed boxes, straightened up and saluted.

"My captain! There is some mistake."

Crepin craned forward, and Burke caught a suppressed oath from him. What the devil did it mean? Suddenly the intelligence officer turned on him fiercely.

"Eh? You, M. Burke—this is incredible! Here. Come with me."

Burke obeyed. Crepin halted him at the roadside, spoke in a low voice.

"Come! You have just one chance. Tell me where they are hidden, or I'll tear the cursed automobile apart!"

"What the devil are you talking about?" demanded Burke.

"The arms and ammunition for El Mekhnezi. I know all about it. Quickly!"

BURKE KNEW that a laugh would ruin him—and suppressed it.

"Crepin—give me your word! Is that why you were after me?"

"You know it damned well," snapped the other. Burke fumbled in his pocket, produced cigarets, struck a match.

"I was offered thirty thousand francs to run that stuff to El Mekhnezi," he said coolly. "That blackguard is a criminal, a murderer, and I'd be the same if I put arms in his hands. I refused."

Crepin started, stood looking hard at him.

"M. Burke," he said in a low voice, "there are some things it is hard to credit."

"I've never broken my word," said Burke gravely. "And I gave my word to El Hanech that tonight I'd bring him a car, with provisions. He wants to get out of the country, over the frontier."

"El Hanech!" exclaimed Crepin sharply. "El Hanech! That poor devil!"

"Exactly. I supposed you wanted to shoot him down—"

"Damnation take you!" cried Crepin angrily. "Am I an assassin of hunted men?"

"You're not far from it. Am I scoundrel enough to give El Mekhnezi guns?"

"Well, you're the next thing to it," snapped Crepin.

Burke broke into a laugh. He could afford it, now.

"Well, you know everything, or nearly everything! But you'll not find out from me where El Hanech is hiding, so save your breath."

Crepin turned to him with a savage oath.

"You've refused to obey orders to halt," he said. "You've damaged government property—you wrecked my car back there! You'll have all sorts of charges against you. Do you realize it?"

"Perfectly. Make the most of it."

"I intend to do so. The court will fine you at least five hundred francs," said Crepin. "Will you give me your word to appear in court tomorrow and answer the charges I shall lay against you?"

"Eh?" said Burke. "Why, of course! But—"

"As soon as my men have replaced that tire of yours, go on with your car," said Crepin harshly. "And tell El Hanech I hope to thunder he gets away safe. Good night."

III

RESCUE

*A Young American Adventurer in Morocco Plays a
Three-Cornered Game with the French Police, Two
Spanish Exiles and a Woman Bent on Vengeance.*

T HE THREE figures by the wall crouched, tense, waiting. Their makeshift *sulhams* of burlap blended perfectly with the brownish wall. It was the hour of evening prayer; from above the Arab city lifted the shrill calls of the muezzins. One of the figures moved slightly. The reflection of lights from the French city glittered on steel.

Denis Burke came striding lithely along, humming a gaily careless air. His lean, erect figure showed clearly. Where the wall turned, he halted abruptly to light a cigarette. The yellow flame of the match flared on his incisive features. At this instant, while the match in his cupped hands blinded him, one of the three figures was upon him with a leap. A curved knife drove in for his stomach.

It did not drive home.

His arms dropped sharply, instinctively, knocking aside the descending sweep of the knife. His head shot forward, colliding with that of the native. The cigarete was thrust into the bearded brown features; a cry of pain burst from the Arab. The other two figures darted in upon the pair.

There was a swift flurry of shapes. Burke slid aside like a shadow; fists thudded in the obscurity under the wall. A knife fell with a tinkle. A choked cry broke on the night, then a hoarse curse burst forth. Abruptly, the tangle of figures disintegrated. There was a slap-slap of slippers, and Burke found himself alone.

He stooped and picked up the fallen knife. It was a very

ordinary curved blade with hammered brass hilt, such as might be bought for a few francs in any bazaar. With a jerk of his hand, Burke flung it over the wall and went his way.

Five minutes later he was sauntering along the Avenue Dar el Makhzene. About him was the glitter and bustle of the great French city that had arisen outside the old walls of Rabat, capital of the new Morocco. Now the usual crowds were redoubled, however, for on the morrow began a week of public audiences with the Sultan. From all parts of Morocco had gathered Berbers and Arabs, chiefs high and low, fakirs, holy men, rascals, officials.

Denis Burke passed beneath a long arched colonnade, dropped in at a *tabac* to buy some matches, and two doors farther on paused to light a cigarette. At his left was a narrow stairway leading to the offices above the line of shops. Standing against the wall, he sent his gaze driving up and down the sidewalk.

He tossed away the match and stepped out to the curb. He might have known it. Crepin himself, no less, head of the intelligence service—an old wolf.

"Ah, M. Burke, a pleasant surprise!"

At the voice, Burke swung around. "Captain Crepin! Faith, I might have known you'd be in Rabat!"

His pleasant, whimsical smile, his dancing blue eyes, gave no indication of his real feelings. Crepin was in mufti as usual, trim, precise, phlegmatic.

"And I," said Crepin calmly, "suspected you would be here. Unwise, isn't it?"

Under that hard, glittering gaze, Burke's brows lifted.

"I fancy not," he said lightly. "I'm here, you know, to give the sultan a petition."

Captain Crepin laughed acidly. "Tell me another," he rejoined. "Even if it were true, you'd not be permitted to approach him. But I know why you're here. You expect to meet agents of

Pequeño in regard to those machine guns awaiting him on the border of the Spanish zone."

"Your mistake," said Burke. "I delivered those guns to Pequeño three days ago."

Crepin's mustache quivered with anger. "What! You have the audacity to admit it?"

"Why not? You can't touch me, Crepin. Besides, I have bigger game afoot than you dream. Running guns? Bah! You have no imagination, my dear fellow. When you discover my real objective here, you'll open your eyes."

"Burke, all personal feelings aside," said the other stiffly, "I warn you that your removal has been ordered. At the first contravention of law on your part, look out!"

Burke clapped the Frenchman on the shoulder.

"Crepin, you're a good sort!" he said warmly. "When your superiors get sufficiently aroused, you'll have to frame me or shoot me, despite yourself. Well, carry on! To the devil with your superiors!"

Captain Crepin shrugged, turned on his heel, and strode away.

AN INSTANT later Burke stepped casually back into the shadow of the colonnade. Then, swiftly, he darted up the narrow flight of stairs, without a sound.

In the hall above, he went directly to a lighted office whose door proclaimed that it belonged to J. M. Marquart, Dentist. Burke tapped lightly. A mustached Frenchman, no other than the dentist, admitted him and beckoned. Burke followed through the outer dental office and came to an inner room.

Here two men in Arab dress sat at a table, and their eyes flashed to him.

"Peace be upon you!" said one, with a grunt.

"And upon you, peace," was Burke's mechanical reply, as he took a chair. "Well, my prediction was correct. Crepin is here. I was just talking with him."

Alarm leaped in the three faces. "You were followed?"

"Not here." Burke chuckled. "I made him so angry that he forgot caution. Now I cannot present the petition."

"Never mind," said one of the Arabs. "I will do that. The reply will be in my hands at ten tomorrow morning; in yours, at noon."

"Good," assented Burke. "Well, Marquart? What news from the outside?"

"I have the money," and Marquart slipped a check across the table. "The share you demanded; fifty thousand francs."

"The ship?"

"I've just had a wireless. She is the *Trinidad*, a small coast passenger ship. She puts in tomorrow night at Casablanca, about midnight, for a couple of hours only, needing fresh water." Marquart grinned. "Her tanks have been fouled, you under-stand. My informant, who is one of the officers, says that the cabins in question are aft, on the port side."

"He must have sent a devilish long message," observed Burke.

"He did. And in code. Precisely half an hour after her anchor goes down, the two men in question will jump. Unless you are ready, they die."

"I'll be ready," said Burke curtly. "Half an hour to the minute, eh?"

"Yes. They will not be able to tell whether you are there."

"Never mind; I shall be there. Go outside, Marquart. I want a private talk."

THE FRENCHMAN shrugged and departed. When the outer door closed, Burke rose, went to the curtain between the rooms, and glanced out. Then he returned, and his blue eyes stabbed at the two Arabs, who gazed at him steadily, impassively.

"Why did three men attack me tonight?" he demanded with abrupt challenge. "You know. Don't lie; or by Allah, I throw up the whole thing here and now!"

Before his fiercely biting eyes, they hesitated.

"Sidi, we are not to blame," said one of them gently. "As Allah liveth, we are—"

"Innocent!" snapped Burke, and spat an oath at them. "You two, and Marquart, alone knew I was coming to Rabat. Yet, five minutes after I parked my car, I was attacked. By Arabs."

The two men exchanged a glance. One made a gesture; the other spoke, obediently.

"Sidi, others knew you were coming. I had a warning tonight about a woman, one whom you yourself had told—"

Burke stared. His lean dark features tensed.

"Impossible! She—the Marquesa—she is herself a relative of those men—"

His voice failed before the impassive gaze of the two Arabs. His thin nostrils quivered; his lips tightened. Yes, he himself was to blame. It was he who had spoken, who had all but betrayed the truth. His shoulders squared.

"I see," he exclaimed. "My friends, you need say no more.

See that the answer of the sultan reaches me at the first possible moment. *Asslama sbah keir!*"

"Good night, sidi," they repeated.

Burke strode from the room. Outside, in the hall, he clapped Marquart on the back and then was gone again to the street—and the woman who awaited him.

II

THE MARQUESA DE GONZAGA had lived in Morocco for five years past; that is to say, two years more than Denis Burke. Her husband had been killed in the Riff campaign.

Allied by birth and marriage with two great Spanish houses, she remained here in Morocco, almost a recluse, occupying a charming little palace in Fez. An extraordinary woman, this. Burke had met her a number of times, but could not understand her. Two days before, he had met her in Fez, had hinted of what was going on. And tonight he was to meet her here in Rabat, at the Transat Hotel. Why should he not have told her, since her own brother and her uncle were the ones concerned.

"But those Arabs knew something!" he thought, as he strode rapidly along the walls of the old Arab city toward the hotel, which lay far from the French town. "They knew! Incredible as it seems, horrible as it may be, they knew! Faith, I'd best look out for her, eh?"

He was appalled by the possibilities of it. Living as he did by his wits, adventurer that he was, conversant with the stark savagery of Moroccan life, this none the less left him chilled and horrified. For he could not doubt.

Fortunately, as yet she knew none of the details.

When Denis Burke reached the hotel, just across from the massive citadel of the Salee rovers, it was barely eight o'clock, just the dinner hour. Burke had no luggage, no evening clothes.

He had come in great haste. All the Transat hotels knew Denis Burke, however, and he had no trouble in getting a room.

A few moments later he descended to the lobby, with its garish imitations of Moroccan decoration, and turned on into the charming salon that adjoined the dining room. Here she was waiting, with a cigarette. She looked up, smiled, extended her hand. Burke bowed over it.

"I nearly despaired of you, and I am hungry," she said, and rose. "Shall we?"

"By all means," assented Burke, and they passed into the dining room, taking one of the small tables by the window. Their order given, her eyes searched him fixedly.

"Well?" she asked. "Is it really true?"

Burke nodded. She could not be a day over thirty-five, he reflected. Once she might have been beautiful; now she was merely hard, proud, unutterably cold. The great lady, yes. One saw this at a glance.

Black hair wound tightly about her head; thin, hard features, cold eyes. No pretense at evening dress, but instead, rough English tweeds. They told queer stories of how she poked around the hills, visiting Berber villages, tramping. And always alone. As though some devil drove her perpetually, the natives said.

"True, yes. If it can be pulled off," Burke replied in English. She spoke it fluently.

"It must be accomplished," she said, leaning forward. "It is the most terrible thing! A hundred or more of the greatest nobles of Spain, crowded into that frightful ship, sent off to exile in that pestilential Rio de Oro—sent off to die of fever! The oldest and greatest blood of Spain, cast into living hell by those republicans!"

YET SHE said this with no show of emotion. Her words were hot, but behind them was no heat. Burke was seeing her now through eyes of suspicion.

"Why would you help any of them to escape?" she demanded suddenly.

"I'm paid for it," said Burke, with a shrug. "Besides, I rather
fancy the idea, Marquesa. There's a lot of fun in circumventing
such deviltry, whether the victims are Spanish grandees or poor
Berber devils. Have you other relatives aboard that hell-ship?"

"No doubt," she answered, "though none of close blood but
my brother, the Conde de Aguilar, and my uncle, the Duc
d'Otranto. How will you manage the escape?"

Did he imagine the cold craft in her eyes? Had he imagined
the slight start of disappointment when she had seen him come
into the salon? Burke could not be sure.

"The plans," said Burke, "are not as I thought. The ship goes
direct to the Rio d'Oro without a stop. Tomorrow I'm going to
Casablanca, catch the first boat down the coast, and arrange
the escape there."

"That will take money," she said. "You must let me help. I
will give you a hundred thousand francs now, more later if you
need it."

"There is no need," said Burke, astonished. "I have received
plenty of money. You can help greatly by letting me bring them
to your house in Fez, if you'll offer it as a refuge to them."

"That goes without saying," she replied. "I shall accompany
you to Rio d'Oro. Perhaps I can be of help there."

"Very well," said Burke. "I leave here at noon tomorrow. Drive
down to Casablanca with me."

So it was arranged. Dinner over, the Marquesa retired to her
room complaining of a headache. Burke left the hotel, strolled
across the street, and waited in the shadow of the trees along
the edge of the Arab cemetery.

Presently, as he had expected, a dark cloaked female figure
left the hotel entrance, and crossing the open space before the
cemetery, plunged into the enormous desolate gateway of the
citadel. After a moment Burke followed. He climbed the steps,
passed through the empty guard chambers, turned into the

street beyond. It was empty. He strode on. Here lived the descendants of those fierce Moors expelled from Spain, who
became the dreaded Salee pirates. Two minutes later, Burke
turned the last corner, and halted.

BEFORE HIM was that enormous gun-platform overlooking the sea, the river-mouth and forts below, where in times
past had thundered cannon at French, Dutch, English fleets.
And there by the low wall was the figure he had followed, and
with it a second.

Even in the starlight, Burke recognized that stiff, square-
shouldered figure at the first glance. It was that of Captain
Crepin. He whistled softly. All doubt set at rest now! She was
betraying him, yes—but why? Betraying, not him alone, but
those two poor devils condemned to a living hell, her own
kinsmen!

Even though he had misled her, she was betraying enough.
Crepin would perceive the truth in a flash; no hope of deceiv-
ing that man! And he would stop everything. The French would
never permit the rescue of those men; French and Spanish
worked together. Still bewildered by the seemingly pointless
treachery of the Marquesa, Burke cursed his own folly in having
opened his mouth to her.

And now everything was lost. Lost, unless—

Denis Burke shrank into the deep shadow of a doorway. The
two figures had turned, were coming toward him. Then they
halted, six feet away.

"Madame, we must not be seen together," said Crepin. "These
natives know everything, see everything. This man Burke would
get warnings from a thousand sources!"

"And you can prevent it?" said the cold voice of the woman.
Burke shivered.

"I can prevent it," replied Crepin. "You have given me what
I need. Now we will take him in the act and turn him over to
Spain. He will be put away quietly—unless he is first killed.
One never knows about these things, madame. This man Burke

is dangerous, a disturbing element, an audacious rascal who stops at nothing."

"Then we have a mutual interest," she said. "You, that Burke be taken care of. I, that they do not escape."

"It is secure in my hands, madame," said Crepin. "Good night."

She departed, passing Burke within arm's reach. Crepin waited, lit a cigarette, then turned and strolled back to the seaward edge of the platform. Burke stood motionless. Temptation drummed at him hideously. This man alone stood between him and success, between him and safety, security, triumph!

With a stifled sigh for his own scruples, Burke left the doorway. He went, not toward the figure on the gun platform, but back along the narrow street to the towering gateway.

After a little, Captain Crepin came walking briskly along the same way. He passed the fountain by the mosque, passed the native café, and came on to the pitch blackness of the unwarded entrance. It swallowed him up. There was a sound; a choked cry, a stir of movement in the darkness, the reiterated thud of fists driving home.

FROM THE inner guard-room ascends a steep and narrow stairs, turning once and coming out on the embattlements. No one ever ventures there, except perhaps a hardy tourist with a guide upon the trail of pirate days.

Burke, with the body of Crepin over his shoulders, toiled up those stairs and came out beneath the stars. He passed along the wall, between its breast-high defenses, to a little round chamber at one corner, where a cannon had once been. There he lowered Crepin and fell to work.

He bound the wrists and ankles of the unconscious man, firmly, but not too tightly. Crepin's handkerchief made an improvised gag, held in place by Crepin's garters. No inarticulate noises would matter.

"Faith, you may guess who's responsible, but you'll never

know!" and Denis Burke chuckled as he rose. "And it won't hurt you to lie here until tomorrow night. Devil a bit! Well, *au revoir!*"

He departed.

Late next morning, Burke encountered the Marquesa in the hotel lobby, and drew her into the little writing room at the side.

"I was looking for you!" he exclaimed eagerly. "Madame, you need not go to Casablanca after all. I am running down there this afternoon to meet a man and obtain full details of an escape that has already been arranged. I shall return tomorrow morning, early. If you will await me here, I'll have news for you!"

She inclined her head coldly.

"Very well," she assented. "I shall be here. I shall be most eager to hear this news. Come to my rooms when you arrive; I have the suite overlooking the citadel."

Burke bowed, and hid the smile that danced in his blue eyes.

It was still a little before noon when an Arab, one of the two he had met in Marquart's office, asked for him at the desk. Burke ordered the Arab brought to his room.

"Peace be upon you!" said the visitor, when the door had closed. "Here is what you desire."

He extended a rolled strip of vellum. Burke unrolled it, glanced at it, and a laugh broke upon his lips.

"Good! Now everything's safe, in spite of the devil himself! Listen—here is something you must do." And he told the other of Captain Crepin's predicament. "Arrange for his discovery and release tonight, but not too early, you comprehend."

"Understood. It will be done. And, sidi, there is something else. I have found that the woman whom you know, hired three ruffians to follow you—"

"Never mind," broke in Burke, his eyes dancing gaily. "Leave that woman to me. Her punishment is my affair."

Half an hour later, he was on his way down the coast to Casablanca.

THE *TRINIDAD* anchored, toward midnight, between the two enormous breakwaters that fend the devouring Atlantic from the *plage* of Casablanca.

Precisely thirty minutes after her anchor-cable roared out, two naked figures dropped from one of her after-ports into the water. Two of that horror-smitten crowd aboard her, the great nobles of Spain, men whose very word had been law, men of wealth and high rank, their heritage the bluest blood of a thousand years, now doomed to a living death in Rio d'Oro.

There was no alarm.

The light boat with its Arab rowers crept in among the bathing-huts of the *plage,* unseen and unheard. The group of men gained the railroad tracks, then the street where Burke's car waited, and separated. Burke and the two naked men got into the car, and he started the engine.

"Clothes, food, wine, all ready for you, gentlemen," he announced cheerfully. "You're free! I have rooms reserved at the Rabat Hotel. We'll be there in an hour or so—only ninety kilometers to go. No speed laws in Morocco, thanks be!"

He was as good as his word.

At nine the next morning, he entered the room where the two fugitives were breakfasting, and greeted them gaily.

"In five minutes, gentlemen, I'm taking you to visit a certain person," he said, "but finish your breakfast. There's no hurry."

He regarded them with interest. The Duc d'Otranto was a man of perhaps fifty, very puffy and paunchy, entirely bald, with a face exactly like that of a vulture—cruel, predatory, with unpleasant eyes. The Conde d'Aguilar was much younger, had a military bearing but not a military face, for there was a certain terror in his eyes, and he overbore Burke with petulant queries about their safety. None the less, these two men had in their veins the bluest blood of Gothic Spain.

Having already apprised the Marquesa of his visit, without mentioning his company, Burke was about to take them to the lady's suite, when a sharp knock came at the door. He opened, saw Captain Crepin and several other men in the passage, and came outside, closing the door behind him.

"Well, Crepin! This is indeed a pleasure."

"None of your *blague*," broke in the other stiffly. "You have had the audacity to bring those men here, to register them under their own names."

"Certainly," exclaimed Burke, with a whimsical smile. "Why not?"

Crepin's moustache quivered. "M. Burke, you have passed the limit. These men are criminals whom you have brought ashore—"

"Political exiles, you mean," said Burke lightly. "How do you know I brought 'em?"

"No matter. They are here, without passports. Their escape has been discovered; the ship is awaiting their return. I must arrest you with them—"

"One minute!" exclaimed Burke. "There is something you do not know, my dear Crepin."

"Indeed?"

"Yes, I assure you. The sultan, I believe, still rules Morocco," and Burke's eyes danced. "He has been pleased to invite the Duc d'Otranto and the Conde d'Aguilar to find shelter in his dominions and to grant them refuge here, and to request me to bring them to his public audience. This will, perhaps, put France in a somewhat delicate position," added Burke gaily, "but after all, the sultan's word is law—"

"Folly!" exclaimed Captain Crepin, but with a startled look in his eyes. "Madness! This is impossible, M. Burke—"

Burke produced the vellum roll and opened it out.

"You read Arabic, of course, my dear Crepin. Cast your eagle glance over this. You know the golden seal of the sultan, naturally."

CREPIN'S FEATURES turned pale as he read the writing there before him.

"Wait!" he snapped. "M. Burke, this affair is not ended and is going to cost you dear. I can still offer you a complete amnesty if we may use the word, on condition that you abandon these two men to the law. Even your assault upon me, the other night—"

Burke chuckled. "We'll discuss that later, my dear Crepin. *Au revoir!*"

Five minutes later, Burke knocked at the Marquesa's door. At her command, he opened, and glanced in. She was sitting in a chair by the window, coldly austere, and Burke bowed to her from the doorway.

"Madame, I wish to introduce two charming friends of mine, whom you know."

And he ushered his two companions into the room.

They were astonished, no less than the woman who sat facing them. Her cold features did not move, but here eyes fastened upon them steadily. Under that quiet, icy gaze the two men bowed, and Otranto turned to Burke. The latter, however, forestalled him.

"Gentlemen, you do not understand, but let me make things clear. Some days ago I met this charming lady and mentioned our little secret, thinking of course that she would be keenly interested. She was," and Burke's eyes drove at her like a sword. "She hired three natives to assassinate me. Failing, she got in touch with Captain Crepin of the Intelligence and betrayed to him as much as she knew. I overheard the conversation," added Burke, "and it was very interesting. She was determined that you two gentlemen should not escape, and while I don't know her reasons—"

Burke paused, in some astonishment.

He had fully expected the Marquesa to be crushed by this revelation of her black treachery toward her own relatives. He had expected the two grandees to overwhelm her with reproaches, with stately Spanish scorn and contumely. To his vast surprise, nothing of the sort happened.

INSTEAD, AGUILAR, who had turned deathly pale, stood staring at the woman with sheer panic heightening in his face. Otranto was wetting his puffy lips and glancing nervously about as though seeking some means of exit.

And the Marquesa, far from being crushed, merely sat there with a slow smile that made Burke's heart contract.

"My dear Mr. Burke," she said calmly, "it is evident that I misjudged your ability. I presume that these gentlemen are quite safe here?"

"Quite," said Burke, and showed the vellum roll. "This gives them refuge and safety, under the hand and seal of the sultan himself. Crepin is absolutely helpless."

"Then, let me tell you what you have done," she began. Otranto intervened, and turned hastily.

"No, no, enough of this!" he cried. "Burke, let us out of here—"

Burke put his hand to the key of the door and turned it.

"Stand quiet," he said grimly. "I've said my say. Madame, proceed, if you please."

"Thank you," she returned, a sudden flash of light in her cold eyes. "You have no doubt wondered why I live in Morocco, far from Spain? Because, when my husband was killed in the Riff campaign, everything went out of my life. Let me tell you how he was—"

Aguilar made a quick, desperate gesture.

"Again?" he croaked. "That old canard? You would fling it in my face?"

"I would," said the woman, with terrible calm. "It is the truth. You commanded his regiment. When you might have saved him, you did not. Instead, you were found crouching in your tent, overcome with terror, a whimpering, abject coward! Thanks to you, he was killed, and thanks to you alone."

"A lie! A lie!" mumbled Aguilar, his face like death. Burke gave him a curious, contemptuous glance.

"Faith, I think it's the truth!" he observed.

"It is," said the Marquesa. "And, once he died, what happened? This grandee of old Castile," and she looked at Otranto, a terrible bitterness in her eyes, "who is my own uncle, seized the entire fortune of my husband, being executor and trustee of the estate. More, he tried to have me shut up in a convent, to keep my mouth closed. I escaped and came to this country, with what I saved of my wealth. Look at him! Hear him deny it!"

Otranto's puffy features were mottled with color.

"My dear—entirely a—a misunderstanding," he said jerkily. "You were misinformed. You—you—blamed me for what others did—"

"I heard you give the orders myself," she said with deadly calm. Otranto swallowed hard. He turned a pitiful, pleading look upon Burke.

"This—this will finish me," he said, agonized. "My heart—"

"Damn your heart," said Denis Burke. "So this is what's behind your actions, madame?"

"Yes," she said, unmoved. "You thought, perhaps, that I was betraying these men. No! But I was willing to go to any length to keep them from evading the punishment that has fallen upon them. Grandees, nobles of Spain, indeed! The one a craven, a coward, who let better men than himself perish horribly while he cowered in his tent. The other a vulture who fed upon carrion, who—"

"Well," said Denis Burke, with a curt laugh, "I have myself to consider here."

Their eyes went to him. He reached behind him and turned the key in the lock again.

IV

"YOU SEE, madame," went on Burke, "I am an Irishman. My ancestors served the Stuarts and many another ignoble person of great blood. There's a fatality in it! May I offer you a cigarette? It will, I assure you, be the most enjoyable cigarette you have ever smoked."

"Thank you," said the woman.

Burke produced cigarettes and crossed to her, extending his case with a bow. The two men stared, uncomprehending, perhaps thinking him mad. She took a cigarette, and Burke did the same, then pocketed the case. He produced matches, and paused.

"There arises a technical question," he said musingly, "but unfortunately I am a gentlemen and not a technician. I accepted fifty thousand francs to rescue these two gentlemen and bring them here. I have done it. Here is the check in question."

He took from his pocket the slip of paper, and with it the vellum letter of the sultan.

"This is the sultan's invitation and safe-conduct, which even the French must respect," he said. "But I forget. Allow me."

He struck a match, leaned forward, held it to her cigarette. Then he held it to his own. Next instant, he held it to the paper and vellum in his hand. The two men did not at once perceive what he was doing.

The paper flared. The vellum curled, burned, smoked fiercely, pervading the room with a hideous smell. A choked cry burst from Otranto, but Burke turned to him with a smile, and the man paused before the look in those blue eyes.

Then, dropping the charred fragments, Burke put his heel on them and went out to find Captain Crepin.

VI

TREACHERY

Burke plays a lone hand in a dangerous game.

D ENIS BURKE was driving his roadster along Highway 14, and he was driving like the devil.

These uplands of Morocco were apparently deserted. Not a house, not a man, was in sight.

From an eminence, Burke looked back. Topping a hill, several miles in his rear, he caught sight of a large car coming furiously. He chuckled, and pressed on the accelerator.

A great top-heavy bus appeared, roaring along from Meknez to Rabat, full within and without, the roof crowded with Arabs and luggage. Burke waved his hand as it passed. Then he dipped into a deep gorge and slowed down for a bridge—one narrow width to serve railroad and vehicles alike. Tires slipping on the hot iron rails, he sped across. Then the roadster roared up the hill beyond and over the crest.

There, beside the road, stood a man in a dirty brown robe. Nothing else was in sight except cactus hedges. Burke slammed on the brakes and leaped out.

"Quickly!" he cried. "They're after me!"

The Arab called sharply. Two other men seemed to rise out of the brown earth. They came running. Burke threw open the luggage compartment of the car. Three long boxes were taken out. The first Arab handed him a roll of thousand-franc notes. Then each of the three picked up one of the heavy boxes, staggering under the weight. Burke drew out his knife, opened it, and deliberately stabbed it into his left front tire. When he turned, the three Arabs and their burdens had vanished completely.

Then, with a roar and a squeal of brakes, the pursuing car plunged to a halt. From it poured half a dozen men—police.

"You are under arrest, Monsieur Burke!" exclaimed the officer in charge. "Your papers!"

"Come, come, my dear sir!" Burke's brows went up in astonishment. "Surely you are jesting! On what charge am I arrested?"

"Illegal possession of arms and ammunition, monsieur," was the crisp retort. "Three boxes in your car. We know they are there; we know all about them!"

"You surprise me, monsieur!" said Burke politely, but with mockery in his eyes. "Undoubtedly you have made a mistake in—"

"We do not make mistakes!" snapped the officer. "We have been trying to catch you for a long time; now we have you red-handed! Men, open up this car! So you fled from us, eh?"

Burke produced a cigarette. "My tire, you observe? It blew out. Fled from you? But how was I to know you were in pursuit of me? Well, well! You are enterprising gentlemen. This is a very pleasant joke, no doubt—"

The officer was aghast, incredulous. His baffled men stared at Burke, for the car was certainly empty.

"Monsieur," said the baffled officer, "somehow you have tricked us. Bah! Let us not mince words. You are playing a game which can have only one end."

Burke bowed. "Thank you, monsieur! So, indeed, it would seem."

White with fury at this response, the officer and his men got into their car, turned about, and headed back for Rabat. Burke remained alone. With a shrug, he got out his jack, and presently had the injured tire replaced by another.

"Cheap at the price!" he reflected comfortably. "One errand done, another remains! And now I'm a trifle late to pick up my passenger. Fortunately, those police were all on the trail of the

rifles and never even scented the big game! Now, if old Crepin had been in command of that party, he'd not have been so dumb."

Crepin, of the Intelligence Department, was a keener antagonist, as Burke knew to his cost. And Crepin had sworn to jail him or expel him from Morocco. Men who ran guns, who were against the government, who helped outlaws, were not liked in this country. Still, Denis Burke had lasted! And he was likely to last even longer. He had plenty of good friends in every city of Morocco, and his wits were seldom dull.

He turned his car around and headed back toward Rabat.

When he came to a dirt road that angled off, he turned and followed it. Two miles, three, then he approached a farm on the left—a miserable native structure, fenced with cactus.

As the car turned in, a native ran to meet it.

"Peace be upon you, sidi!" he exclaimed, recognizing Burke.

"And upon you," echoed Burke, who was puzzled. "Where is El Mokri?"

"But, sidi! Your messenger got him, two hours ago!"

"I sent no messenger. Explain!"

The native fell silent in abrupt consternation. El Mokri, outlaw and rebel, on whose head was a price of two thousand francs, had awaited Burke here. Arrangements had been prepared. El Mokri, if caught by the French, was a doomed man. But if he could first reach the sultan in Rabat and obtain a pardon, he was saved. Relatives had handled the affair. The sultan had signified that, if El Mokri fell at his feet as he entered his private mosque, and begged pardon and forgiveness, all would be well. Burke had the job of getting him there past vigilant French eyes, and he was to pocket ten thousand francs for the service.

"Sidi," gasped the native, "a man came in an automobile, saying you had sent him. El Mokri went with him, and this was two hours ago. As—"

"We are betrayed," said Burke. "Describe this man, quickly!"

The farmer, who was also a relative of the outlaw, had missed nothing.

"An ordinary Bitroen car, sidi. The man was tall, thin, a Frenchman. He wore blue overalls, a brown shirt, and the cap of a mechanic. He had a black mustache, waxed at the ends; his age was perhaps thirty-five."

"Did he have heavy black eyebrows, one more arched than the other?"

"He did. Then you know him?"

"I know him," said Burke grimly. "Farewell! Leave things in my hands."

He turned his car about and drove away like mad, heading back for Rabat.

Yes, he knew the man! Georges Delacroix, a shrewd shyster lawyer, had been in Morocco for years. He was mixed in every kind of rascality, he stopped at nothing to gain his ends.

"What's his game, and who's behind him?" thought Burke, as he drove. "To pick a fight with me, he must have backing! Is he turning El Mokri over to the French? So! Now I see the explanation of what happened—some one has betrayed us, eh? Planned to get me pinched and out of the way. Delacroix figured he'd remove me and step into my boots, all at one crack! Well, he miscued, that's all!"

A FEW minutes after five he drove across the bridge, with the French and Arab cities of Rabat before him. Ahead and on his left loomed the great red Tower of Hassan, that relic of past ages. He glanced at it and passed on, going directly to his hotel, the France, in the French city.

Entering, he inquired for messages. He was handed a telegram, tore it open, and read:

QUARTER TO SIX STOP TOWER OF HASSAN
ISMAIL

Burke glanced at his watch. Good! Turning from the hotel, he strode rapidly along, cutting down to the Rue du Capitaine Petitjean, which would lead him back to the ancient tower near the river. So Ismail knew something. It was Ismail who had arranged things with the sultan—a shrewd old rascal who would not even allow himself to meet Burke in any ordinary manner.

Cutting in to the Tower of Hassan by one of the paths from the street, Burke found no one in sight. He went direct to the tower, and a voice called him to the foot of the ancient stairs. There he found Ismail, hooded, stooped over a staff, only beard and two glittering eyes visible.

"So you are safe, sidi!" exclaimed the Arab.

"No fault of yours," snapped Burke. "You know about Delacroix, do you?"

"Allah curse him! He is working with the Caid Ali, sidi. He brought El Mokri to his own villa in the Avenue des Touargas, not far from the palace of the sultan, on whom be blessings! To-night the caid will go there."

Dennis Burke was silent. So this explained it—Caid Ali! A bad enemy there. He was a wealthy man, related to the grand vizier, powerful at the sultan's court, deep in intrigue and graft. The combination with Delacroix made an unpleasant team.

"El Mokri was not a party to it?"

Ismail cackled. "Scarcely, since he is to be tortured to-night! The caid wants to make him tell where his treasure is buried, before turning him over to the French. They are old enemies, sidi."

"Who betrayed us?"

"My nephew."

"Said, eh? What do you propose to do about it?"

"Nothing, sidi. Said is dead."

Used as he was to callous Morocco, these words appalled Burke. The traitor nephew dead—slain, no doubt, by this man before him!

"Allah will pardon," murmured Burke, thinking fast. "What chance of rescuing El Mokri?"

"None, sidi, unless we tell the police where he is, to save him."

"No. What hour was he to meet the sultan?"

"At the sunrise prayer, sidi—about six in the morning at this season."

"Very well," said Burke. "Can you discover within the next half hour how the caid will go to the villa of Delacroix, and at what hour?"

"He will go in his automobile, no doubt. I can learn the exact hour."

"Do so. Telephone me at the hotel as soon as you find out. Delacroix has other men with him at the villa?"

"Two, sidi. The Russian, Orloff, and Henri Sorbier, the Algerian. But he is not there now. He is dining with a lady."

Burke started. "Dining with a lady! Are you certain?"

"Yes, sidi. I have had men watching him ever since I learned of this treachery. He has engaged a private room at the Petit Poucet; so it is not likely that the caid will go to his house very early."

"Excellent!" exclaimed Burke. "Telephone me within half an hour; after that, I shall be away."

BACK AT his hotel, Burke dressed in haste, but carefully. All that could save El Mokri, and with him the reputation of Dennis Burke in native eyes, was audacity and swift action. He donned his dinner jacket and was ready to leave when the telephone message came from Ismail. Just one word: "Nine!" This meant that the caid was due at the Delacroix villa at nine. The time was now well past seven. Then the voice of the old Arab went on:

"One thing more. I understand that Captain Crepin reached town this evening."

With this, Ismail rang off abruptly. Burke whistled softly. Crepin's presence boded trouble. With Crepin in charge, there would be no more bungling.

Burke hesitated, glanced around the room. They were out to get him now; treachery and betrayal, once begun, would spread like wildfire. Perhaps some Arabs among his own friends and clients were out to supplant him by Delacroix! Well, the man had chosen his role. It was a struggle to the death—or jail—between them.

Here were the papers on the Filali rifle affair, as yet uncompleted; a matter of ten or twelve thousand francs only. If they were after him, if this were betrayed, then Crepin would search Burke's room. Neglect nothing! Burke sat down and fell to work. The papers alone could not harm him, were his name not involved. With acid, razor blade, and ink, he changed the name beyond any possibility of its recognition. This done, he stuffed the papers in a wastebasket and grinned.

Then, whistling cheerily, he took up hat and stick and sauntered out of the hotel in all the glory of his evening attire.

The Petit Poucet was a rambling structure built circularly about a tiled court, in native style. There were public rooms, private rooms, all sorts of rooms imaginable. Burke did not enter, but took a table on the sidewalk outside and beckoned a waiter who had served him before.

"A bock, Emile," he said, slipping the other a hundred-franc note, "and the number of the private room occupied by Monsieur Delacroix. The name of his companion, also. It is an affair of the heart."

Delighted by this intimate confidence, Emile scurried away. He was gone for some time, then returned with the bock and wiped the table carefully.

"Number eleven, m'sieu'," he murmured. "And Madame Desfarges."

Burke nodded, and drank his bock unhurried, a smile on his lips. Madame Desfarges, eh? A clever widow, undeniably charming, this lady had contacts in surprising quarters and made the most of them. It was she, for example, who had negotiated with Burke for all those rifles for the Filali Berbers.

"And now she is selling me out, eh?" reflected Burke. "Excellent! I shall not interfere with her in the least. However—"

He rose and entered the Petit Poucet. He knew his way about here, as he did in most corners of Morocco.

Burke sauntered casually into Room 11 on the second floor.

Then he closed the door behind him and turned the key in the lock.

They sat staring at him in absolute silence for a long moment—the man and the woman sitting behind the table. Madame Desfarges was slender, baby-faced, golden of hair and green of eye; her cheeks drained of color as she watched Burke.

Delacroix was startled enough. His black eyes, beneath uneven, bushy brows, narrowed in alarm; but forcing an appearance of ease, he thumbed his waxed mustache and broke the silence.

"Ah, Monsieur Burke! Do you always enter unannounced?" Burke bowed.

"Madame, a thousand pardons! I regret to intrude, but I must ask you to leave us for a few moments. It is imperative that I speak with Monsieur Delacroix."

"On what subject, if you please?" inquired the man, obviously surprised.

"A private matter. I might say that Orloff told me where to find you."

DELACROIX WAS cautious enough, but this cordiality, this utter lack of any accusation or anger, gave him pause. He had not the slightest reason to think that Burke knew of his activities. Besides, the hand he had slipped beneath his coat rested on the pistol there, and he feared nothing.

"Perhaps, *cherie,* you had better leave us," he said quietly. The woman rose, and without a word obeyed. Burke unlocked the door and held it open, bowing low as she passed. Then he closed and locked it again, and turned.

"What the devil!" exclaimed Delacroix. "Are you afraid of intruders?"

"Precisely. The police are seeking everywhere for me." Burke came forward. In his excited eyes, in his words, was urgent haste.

"I've no time to lose! They've seized my car, they have seized my room, my papers, my very clothes!" he went on. "My native friends warned me, too late, to get away. Now they will not help me. I have money enough, but I need clothes and, perhaps, a car. I must cross the frontier before dawn. You understand?"

Delacroix's eyes glittered with exultation, with rapid calculation. So Burke had been caught off guard! Better to help him get away, or let him stay? Help him, of course. Delacroix had no desire for a show-down with this man.

"But, my friend, what can I do?" he murmured, producing cigarettes, lighting one, and extending his case. Burke refused.

"Provide me with a change of clothes and a car. I'm in danger every minute here!"

Delacroix forgot about his pistol now. He glanced at his watch and frowned.

"There is a two-seater that you might have, certainly. Orloff could provide you with clothes and food. But what if the frontier is closed to you?"

"I'll chance that," said Burke quickly. "It's only a hundred and sixty kilometers to El Ksar, on the frontier, and I'm safe enough there."

The dark eyes flashed. Better and better! Let the fellow get away, let him go clear, and then warn the police! He would be caught like a rat in a trap at El Ksar!

"Very well," exclaimed Delacroix, with decision. "Here, have a glass of wine—"

Several bottles stood on the table. Delacroix filled a glass, pushed it at Burke, then took out notebook and pencil. On a page of the notebook he wrote in French:

Orloff:
Give Monsieur Burke whatever he needs in the way of clothes. Put provisions in the Genault, see that it is filled with petrol, and turn over the car to him.
                    DELACROIX.

He tore out the sheet and extended it to Burke.

"Give this to Orloff; he knows my writing."

Burke rose, leaned over the table, and took the paper in his left hand. His right caught up an empty bottle and brought it down across Delacroix's head.

The Frenchman slumped across the table.

Catching hold of him, Burke dragged his limp form out on

the floor, took his pistol, notebook, money, and other papers, then tied him hand and foot with napkins from the table. Another napkin knotted about his mouth, and it was done. He rolled the unconscious man beneath a divan, where he was well out of sight, then went to the door, unlocked and opened it. Pausing only to light a cigarette, he stepped out into the hall.

Madame Desfarges was approaching from the stairway. With a smile and an uneasy glance, she came to the open door, glanced into the room, and turned.

"Where is he?"

Burke's brows lifted. "Did you not see him, madame? He said he would let you know at once that he was called away—"

"You devil!" she broke out, turning pale. "What have you done?"

"But I do not comprehend!" said Burke. "Is it my fault if he had to leave suddenly? Come, my dear madame, allow me to see you home."

With an angry exclamation, she flung her wrap about her shoulders and departed. Burke chuckled to himself, and followed, unhurried.

Ten minutes later he was at the door of Delacroix villa in the Avenue des Touargas.

ORLOFF WAS an intellectual Russian refugee, a type common in north Africa. He was slender, nervous, entirely on the alert. Not until he had read the note from Delacroix, did he admit Burke into the house. Then he called Sorbier.

The villa was plainly furnished, but of some size, having two stories. The Algerian appeared at the call. He was a rat-faced little man of pronounced criminal type.

"Monsieur Burke," said Orloff, "this is Monsieur Sorbier. I will go and get the car filled and ready. Sorbier, orders are that Burke be given anything in the way of clothes that he needs. Best take him into the bedroom of Monsieur Delacroix and give him his choice."

"Upstairs, m'sieu'," said Sorbier. Burke caught a glance that the two exchanged, and read it aright. They suspected nothing; however, Sorbier was on his guard. No time to lose with him, therefore.

Passing to the hall, Burke preceded the Algerian up the narrow stairs to an upper hall. Here Sorbier took the lead, threw open a door, and switched on the lights in a bedroom. He motioned Burke to enter, and followed. Going to a closet, Sorbier opened the door.

"Here, m'sieu', look for yourself—ah! Name of a name—"

Then he fell silent, his hands lifting. The pistol in Burke's hand was pressed against his stomach, and the look in those chilling gray eyes fairly froze him.

In five minutes Burke had his victim trussed up and had found at the end of the corridor the room he sought.

A feeble groan sounded as he switched on the lights. On the bed, tied wrist and ankle to each corner post, was El Mokri, cruelly gagged, eyes rolling. On his lean, bearded face was blood and his brown robe was ripped and torn. At one side, evidently placed ready for use, was an electric grill, with two soldering irons. Then he darted to the bedside.

"So they slipped one over on us, El Mokri!" he said cheerfully, as he sawed with his knife at the cords of the gag. "We haven't met for a year or so, but you're the lone wolf of the hills, right enough. Well, Ismail is waiting for you, and I got here two jumps ahead of your friend the caid, and you're to see the sultan in the morning—"

El Mokri spat out an oath and the remnants of the gag, but for a little had no use of his hands, so tightly had he been bound. At this moment, Burke leaped up, started for the door, hearing a step in the hall. As he threw open the door, he came face to face with Orloff, who, unluckily for himself, had not expected this meeting. Burke's fist crashed into his face and sent him reeling.

Even so, it was a close thing. Orloff whipped out a knife and

the wickedly curved steel came within an ace of disemboweling
Burke. Then the Russian whimpered, dropped his weapon,
staggered back. He cried out in agony and flung both arms
about his face as hard fists thudded into him. At this, Burke
hit him twice under the belt and then dragged the senseless
figure back into the bedroom.

El Mokri, sitting up, smiled grimly.

"By Allah, I will slit the throat of this dog!" he observed.
Burke grinned.

"No. Your job is to reach Ismail's house. Can you do it?"

"Here in the city I am safe enough."

"Then clear out. We've not a minute to spare."

Reluctantly, El Mokri complied with the order. Burke led
him downstairs and saw him off. Then, switching on the porch
light of the villa, he stood beneath it, watching the street. Presently he lighted a cigarette and sauntered out to the curb, as an
automobile turned the corner and slowed down.

The car halted. Burke opened the door, sighted two natives
within.

"Don't get out, Caid Ali," he said pleasantly. "The man you
seek is gone. Monsieur Delacroix accepted a larger sum than
you offered."

"Allah curse you!" came the angry response. "Is this true?
Who are you?"

"His agent." With a laugh, Burke closed the car door and
turned to the driver. "Back to the native city—and hurry!"

He gayly tipped his hat after the departing car, and strode
away. A perfect evening's work! Delacroix set at naught, his
enemies baffled, El Mokri safe and free—

As Burke turned the corner, the heavens seemed to fall upon
him.

BURKE WAKENED to glowing sunlight which came
through high windows and lighted a room where shimmering,

ancient tiles covered the floor and the walls to the height of a man.

On the table before his eyes was a modern telephone. And sitting beside it was Madame Desfarges, regarding him with a smile.

Burke wakened slowly. His head hurt, his brain was heavy with drug fumes; he had been knocked down and then drugged. Spread out on the table, he saw everything that he had taken from the pockets of Delacroix—notebook, papers, letters, money.

"I see you admire my house," said the woman. "Pray make yourself comfortable."

Burke realized where he was, for madame occupied a charming little palace in Medina, the native city. He tried to move, and looked down. He was sitting in a huge chair, whose heavy wooden arms were clamped down across his wrists. It was one of those ancient chairs in which men sat unsuspecting, to find themselves suddenly prisoners.

The telephone bell rang sharply. Madame Desfarges answered it.

"Ah! So you received my message, Monsieur Delacroix!" she exclaimed. Her glance drove mockingly at Burke. "Yes, I know where he is. Also, I have the notebook and letters he took from you. What? Fifty thousand francs a ridiculous sum? Very well.... No, you cannot see me this morning. You will not be admitted. Au revoir."

A calculating smile in her eyes, she called a number, and waited.

"Ah, Caid Ali! This is Madame Desfarges.... Yes, I have here a number of papers and a notebook, also letters, taken from Monsieur Delacroix late night. Two of the letters are from you, in connection with the operation of the customs service at Ujda, which is your charge. Also, you are mentioned frequently in the notebook. What is more, I know where Monsieur Burke is at this moment, if you would care to put your hands on him...

Oh! My dear caid, such language in a man of position! Would you be interested to the extent of fifty thousand francs, within the next hour?… Absurd? Very well, thank you."

She rang off abruptly and turned the battery of her slow smile upon Burke.

"And you?" she asked. "Perhaps you would like some coffee? Akbar!"

She clapped her hands, and a native servant entered, received her instructions, and departed. Burke said nothing. Presently the native returned with a tray arranged with a coffee service. When they were alone again, Madame Desfarges poured coffee, brought it to Burke, held it to his lips. He swallowed it, hot as it was.

"Thank you, madame. Why not try selling me to Captain Crepin?"

"Ah! The Intelligence has no money to spend, dear Monsieur Burke, and I want to be on my way to Paris to-night, you comprehend. Caid Ali has evidently found out about your doings of last night; he is furious. Still, you yourself should be able to bid."

"By all means," Burke assented. The telephone rang, and she responded.

"Oh, Monsieur Delacroix again? You offer thirty thousand? I am not interested. You need not ring me again, m'sieu'. Send a messenger with the money, and if no one else has accepted my terms, well and good. That is your risk. Adieu!"

She rang off and gave Burke an eager glance. "Well? Fifty thousand?"

"Yes," said Burke quietly.

"For your liberty alone, mind! These Delacroix articles are not included."

"Agreed. Would you kindly give me a cigarette and light it? Ah! Thank you. One thing, madame, how do you know I would not endeavor to revenge myself upon you?"

She laughed a little. "I shall be in Paris. Also, you will give me your word. You are a gentleman; these others are rascals. And I shan't release you until noon."

Burke smiled. "Very well. I see my check book on the table there."

She brought the check book and a fountain pen to his lap, left them, and drew a small brass key from her gown; it was hung on a chain about her neck. Introducing it in the right-hand arm of the chair, she turned it and then stepped behind the chair. Burke tried to free his arm, and the heavy carved wood lifted easily to the effort.

He had no choice, he knew well; he was caught, and freedom was cheap at the price. With some effort, he managed the one-hand job, writing out the check. Then, at her order, he laid his hand on the arm rest. She swung down the heavy wood, and he was again a captive. Laughing, she caught up the pen and check book and resumed her seat.

"The bank will not open till ten," she observed. "However, I can discount this with one Ismail—I believe he knows your signature. An excellent idea!"

She left the room. After she closed the door, Burke heard the key turn in the lock.

BURKE GAVE his whole body a heave and a wrench. His feet were free; the chair slid a little on the smooth tiles of the floor. Inch by inch, the chair moved. The table was not large. It was a taboret of slender carved wood inlaid with shell. After a little, Burke put out his foot, hooked it about one leg of the table, and slid it over to him.

Then he tipped up the table, carefully. The papers and note-book slowly slid off to the floor. The telephone slipped, then Burke tipped the table toward him. With a sharp, abrupt pitch, the telephone fell into his lap, the receiver came off its rack. Immobile now, leaning forward, Burke caught the voice of central.

"Hello! Emergency call, mademoiselle! Prefecture of police, if you please."

A man's voice clicked up at him. Burke demanded Captain Crepin of the Intelligence Department, and to his delight heard the dry accents of Crepin issue:

"Hello, Crepin! This is Burke speaking. I am in serious trouble in the palace occupied by Madame Desfarges. If you will get here quickly, you'll grab letters and papers inculpating Caid Ali, Delacroix, and possibly others in customs frauds. I'm locked in a sunken room, probably just off the court."

"Thank you, m'sieu'," came the dry response, then silence. Burke let the instrument slide off on the floor, and resigned himself to waiting.

He understood that Madame Desfarges had herself gone to discount his check with old Ismail, which meant that she might be gone much or little time.

Half an hour passed in silence. There was a clock on the wall at one side. Burke eyed it fiercely; dismay seized him on realizing that an hour, a full hour, was gone! The minutes seemed eternal. The woman had not returned, yet she had counted on leaving at once!

The sharp click of steps sounded on the tiles. Then the key turned in the lock, and the door swung open. On the threshold stood Captain Crepin, with several other men behind him. They stood staring into the room.

"Well?" exclaimed Burke angrily. "You've been long enough coming here! I offered you a good price for freedom—why the devil didn't you come sooner?"

He fell silent, puzzled. Crepin conferred with the others, then spoke to one of them.

"Here is the key. Touch nothing; let us look first at his wrists."

They came forward. The man with the key—the little brass key, still on its chain—unlocked the chair arms. Crepin gestured Burke to be quiet.

"Do not rise, if you please. Let us see your wrists—ah!"

Burke, who was still in evening dress, showed his wrists. Although mystified, he noted that the ridges in his skin and flesh, where the oak edges had bitten into him, were what drew the interest of all. A nod was exchanged, then Crepin turned to him.

"Monsieur, the papers which you mentioned over the telephone—"

"Are here on the floor. What the devil does all this mean, Crepin? How did you get hold of that key? Last I saw it, the thing was around madame's neck."

"Indeed?" Crepin surveyed him coolly. "There is no doubt, from the marks on your wrists, that you have been here at least an hour or more—that is to say, since you telephoned me. May I ask you, monsieur, whether you own a rather large knife with a silver handle, on which your name is engraved?"

"Eh?" Burke frowned. "Yes, of course I do. I don't carry it with evening clothes. It is in my room at the Hotel de France. What about it?"

Crepin turned to one of the other men. "You have just come from his room. Well?"

"No knife there, Captain Crepin. The room was in the utmost disorder; it had clearly been entered and searched. No papers of any consequence except these, which I found in the wastebasket."

From him Crepin took the crumpled papers relating to the rifle deal, and cast an eye over them.

"Ah! I see these papers bear the name of Delacroix," murmured Crepin. He met the eyes of Burke, and smiled slightly. "At all events, monsieur, there is nothing against you. You are a very lucky man. I congratulate you with all my heart on being locked up here!"

"Why?" demanded Burke.

"Because, forty-five minutes ago, Madame Desfarges was murdered in the narrow Rue d'Ismail," said Crepin gravely. "No one saw the act committed. She was killed by two deep stabs in the throat—and the knife remained. It was your knife."

Burke started. His own knife! Then some one had ransacked

his room at the hotel, had taken the knife, had murdered the woman, probably after she had cashed his check—either agents of Delacroix or agents of Caid Ali! He swiftly told what had happened to him, told of her telephone messages. Crepin and his men nodded. They glanced at the notebook, at the letters. Then Crepin smiled.

"No European had been seen in the Rue d'Ismail preceding the crime," he said quietly. "I think we shall question Caid Ali about this murder—about this, and these other things as well. As to Delacroix—well, there will be charges enough against him. Monsieur Burke. Once more, you are free."

"Thank you." Burke rose, and accepted the cigarette Crepin held out. "By the way, there was a native servant here. If he had been listening, he might have overheard the talk here; he might even have followed and murdered Madame Desfarges, knowing of the sum she would be bringing back!"

Crepin smiled thinly. "That servant, m'sieu', is already in custody. He proved to be a nephew of Caid Ali. His finger prints are being compared with those found on the silver handle of the knife."

"The devil!" exclaimed Burke. "Then—"

The intelligence officer shrugged. "Treachery, my dear Monsieur Burke, is a rather risky game to play in Morocco! As to that knife, it will be returned to you later, of course."

Burke shook his head.

"No, thanks. I don't want it," he said, and went back to his hotel.

VI

INVITATION TO A CRIME

Denis Burke accepts, from the police,
an Invitation to a Crime.

DENIS BURKE was enjoying a cigar and a drink on the terrace of the Café de Paris, in the new French city of Meknez. At the moment he had no pressing business, and could survey the Moroccan scene calmly.

Then he straightened a trifle. No mistaking that trim, erect figure heading across the sidewalk! Captain Crepin, chief of the intelligence bureau.

"Ah, Crepin! Faith, I thought you were in Marrakesh!" exclaimed Dennis Burke, as the other halted and nodded. "Sit down. Take your mind off criminals and enjoy a drink!"

To his astonishment, Crepin accepted the invitation. They exchanged a few words, Crepin bit at a cigar, and his drink arrived. Then he fastened his intent, stern gaze upon Burke and leaned forward, speaking distinctly but very softly.

"Mon ami, I have often wished you were out of this country!"

Burke laughed. "And vice versa, my dear Crepin! You've done your best to make life interesting for me. And I've done my best to repay the compliment."

Crepin grimaced. "True. You have influence among the natives; they all know you. We French are rather helpless—we can't catch you red-handed. You run guns, you respect few laws, and you have the devil's own audacity. You are a nuisance."

"Thank you," observed Burke, but his gray eyes narrowed. "I seem to get away with it, eh?"

Crepin shrugged. "However, we hold each other in a certain

respect, Monsieur Burke. You may be a thorn in the side of the government; but you are a gentleman, and—"

"What's on your mind, besides me?" Burke interrupted.

"Haven't you heard about Captain Latrobe?"

"I know Latrobe well, a fine chap!" exclaimed Burke. "What about him? I just got into town half an hour ago. When I saw you, I thought you were trailing me."

Crepin smiled thinly.

"Not this time; but I am glad to see you. Let us forget enmities. You can help me, if you will."

Utterly astounded at this, Burke frowned over his cigar.

"You are serious, Crepin? Your pardon; you are always serious. What's this about Latrobe?"

"He was murdered last night, precisely at midnight, in his own quarters. A native knife, a trophy that belonged to him, was driven through his neck from behind."

"The devil!" Burke was shocked by the news. Latrobe, a splendid officer, a splendid man—murdered! "Who did it?"

"Don't be absurd. Not a native, assuredly, because no native had access to the officers' quarters except orderlies, and none of them was around at midnight."

Burke whistled. "Therefore an officer! Not so good. How do you know he was murdered at midnight?"

"He went to his own room at nine, to write letters. He was not seen again. He was killed while sitting at his table, writing. His watch, lying on the table before him, had been knocked to the floor and broken, obviously at the time of the murder. Midnight."

"Finger prints?"

"None. We overlooked nothing, of course."

"You're extremely wet," said Burke, abruptly. "He wasn't killed at midnight. That stoppage of a watch is an elementary sort of trick! Probably he was killed between nine and ten. I'll wager he didn't have a big pile of letters written!"

Captain Crepin started. "That is true. One letter finished, another begun! But that is not all; I have not told you the worst. Latrobe was head of the commission making a report on the new chain of posts to be established in the Atlas. That report was in his pocket, he had just finished correcting it. Now it is gone! And you know what it means if our whole plan of occupation and forts and defenses comes into the hands of the Berbers!"

"Faith," said Burke, "if I had the thing, I know where I could get a hundred thousand francs for it within three days!"

"I'll wager you do," said Crepin, regarding him intently. "Well, set a thief to catch a thief! You will pardon the allusion. You are in touch with all the outlaws in the country. Will you undertake the recovery of this report and, if possible, the finding of poor Latrobe's murderer?"

"How do you know I wouldn't recover the report and keep it for my own purposes?"

"More absurd questions! You'll give me your word, and it is good."

"My dear Crepin, I've no sympathy with your administration. Why should I help you? No!"

"Then you refuse?"

"To help you? Absolutely!" said Burke. "I wouldn't lift my hand to help all the police in Africa! However, to avenge poor Latrobe is another matter. He was my friend. One of your rotten officers with friends in the senate, relatives in the ministry, a pull all along the line, has probably done him in. Did he have enemies?"

"None that we can discover," answered Crepin.

"All right." Burke nodded, then lifted his glass. "I'll do my best. You have my word! But at a price. Pay first, Crepin."

The intelligence officer frowned. "How much?" he demanded crisply.

"One Abdallah."

"Eh? I don't understand—"

Burke grinned. "You have my friend Abdallah ben Sus here in Meknez, in jail, awaiting trial. You missed me, but caught him after I had delivered the machine guns to him. Well, turn him loose immediately! If you don't, you'll never see or hear of that report again. If you do, then I'll do my best! Yes or no?"

"You have the devil's own nerve!" said Crepin angrily. He caressed his quivering mustache, caught Burke's eye and his anger died. "All right, it's agreed! A truce is declared between us—eh?"

"Agreed. Now, is there any one whom you might suspect? Did Latrobe have an orderly? Did he have any disreputable friends?"

"No. His native orderly has an excellent record, and in any case is away on sick leave." Crepin hesitated. "There is one person—however, to my positive knowledge he has been away from barracks for three days, drunk and gambling—young Courtot."

"Oh! I know him slightly," and Burke frowned. "Dissolute rascal, eh? You're sure about him? He's to—"

"He's facing court-martial," said Crepin. "I looked him up. Dead drunk all last night in a gambling villa outside town."

Burke shrugged, and lifted his glass. "Well, here's luck!"

CLOSE TO eight o'clock Denis Burke returned to the Transatlantique, where he was stopping. He beckoned one of the young Arab guides, and the native followed him into the writing room.

"I wish two messages delivered immediately in the native city," said Burke. "I'll pay well. Do you want to do it or not?"

"Yes, sidi."

"Very well. Sit down and write in Arabic. Don't make any changes or errors, for I'll know it."

The youth seated himself, and Burke dictated:

> "Last night a manuscript report was stolen from the quarters of Captain Latrobe. I am in the market if it can be delivered to me before midnight to-night.
> "Denis Burke, Transatlantique Hotel."

Burke inspected the Arabic writing and nodded.

"Make a copy. Take one to Hassan ben Daoud, whose house you know. The other goes to Sidi Ahmed el Barak. Here's your money. Lose no time about it!"

He crossed the lobby and entered the dining room. He took his accustomed table by a window.

Burke was confident that he would get swift results. He did not doubt that some officer had murdered Latrobe and stolen the report.

"If this is the case," he reflected, "the negotiations for its sale would not be concluded before sometime to-night. And certainly, nobody will suspect me!"

Only too true. Burke was known far and wide as being against the government.

It was a toss-up between the two men whom he had written. Hassan was agent for many Berber tribes, a smooth politician. Sidi Ahmed was very different. He was wealthy, owned race horses and gambling dives. He knew all the criminals in Morocco, had a position at the sultan's court. Nothing was too low, nothing too exalted, if he stood to profit by it.

If nothing developed from these two, the Arab guide who had written the message would have spread its contents all over Meknez within an hour's time. So Burke went to dinner, supremely unconcerned with the outcome. If money were an issue, no one concerned would have the slightest hesitation in dealing with him.

Burke was far from prepared, however, for what actually happened.

He had finished dinner and had gone to his room, when he was summoned to the telephone in the hotel lobby. One telephone to a hotel is the French limit. When he reached the instrument, he was greeted by a woman's voice.

"Monsieur Burke?... This is Madame Desaix.... You must pardon my call, but I wish to know whether you sent a certain note this evening to Sidi Ahmed."

"Eh? Oh, yes!" exclaimed Burke, thinking fast. "Yes, I did."

"Then will it be agreeable if I send my car for you in twenty minutes?"

"With all my heart, madame!" he responded cheerily. "I have long desired the honor of your acquaintance."

With a laugh, she rang off. Burke swore softly to himself.

Madame Desaix—so she was in cahoots with Sidi Ahmed! She was well enough if not favorably known; a Russian woman who had married a French officer years before, was now a widow, and had a gorgeous villa on a hill outside of town.

A thousand questions tormented Burke, but he was forced to dismiss them. That the woman would have Latrobe's report was unlikely in the extreme; it was too compromising. Nor did its value lie in military details, but in commercial possibilities.

To know in advance where all the new French forts would lie—

Burke stiffened, then broke into a whistle as the woman's probable scheme flashed into his mind. He realized how she would play her game! The man who had the document would come to her villa, would deal through her as agent. Sidi Ahmed might be there in another room; he would have purchasers for that information. Burke would be there; one would bid against the other!

Where, then, could the manuscript be? Probably hidden somewhere; no officer would take chances with such evidence. It would be hidden. A messenger would be sent for it.

A glance at his watch, and Burke strolled out to the entrance. He was standing there when a roadster with an Arab driver rolled up. The Arab opened the door, saw him.

"Monsieur Burke? Very good."

IN COMPLETE silence, they drove to the outskirts of the French city, turned off a road between two iron gates in a wall, and came to a halt beside a rather pretentious structure amid gardens. The house was glittering with lights. An Arab in gorgeous costume opened the door. Burke was disappointed to find the place apparently empty.

Then he turned. Madame Desaix was approaching, hands outstretched.

"I am enchanted, madame!" he murmured. His gray eyes met hers with friendliness. "And to think that we only meet because of business!"

"Come, come, my friend! We have no time for pretty speeches which you do not mean," she said firmly. "I know all about you—especially that you are impervious to women. Well, let us confine ourselves to business! Come into the little salon, where we may be alone. You will not refuse mint tea?"

Burke was too much taken aback to refuse anything. He certainly had not expected this sort of a greeting!

She led him into a charming little salon that held only three chairs, a table, and a tabouret where an Arab servant placed a silver tray. Upon it were goblets of the mint tea that Arabs love. Burke glanced at the table, with a telephone and a Paris magazine, noticed that the door was closed fast, then gave his attention to the woman before him.

"Why do you want the Latrobe report?" she demanded. Burke smiled, producing cigarettes.

"My business is my own, madame," he replied pleasantly.

"And mine is mine, Monsieur Burke. I know where to get it! I may arrange the purchase. The document is not secret. The information—"

"Bah! Stop fencing," said Burke. "I'm bidding against Sidi Ahmed, is that it? What is the highest bid he can afford on behalf of those whom he represents?"

"One hundred fifty thousand francs," she replied.

"I'll give one seventy-five—cash," said Burke, and lighted his cigarette.

She caught her breath, then picked up her tea and sipped it.

"You haven't that sum in cash with you?"

"No more than you have the document I want, madame. But I, like you, can get it."

"I shall need the money to-night, within the hour."

"You shall have it as soon as the bargain is assured."

"Wait here, please."

She rose and went to the door, which opened on a central hall, with a stairway at the end to the right. Burke rose gallantly and went to the door, opening it for her. She passed with a word of thanks. He perceived that the hall was empty, and then shut the door hard, but kept the knob from turning. Next instant he pushed the door open the merest trifle and looked out. She was turning at the stairs. Burke went back to the table and pressed out his cigarette.

"Give her thirty seconds," he muttered. "She's going upstairs.

But why? Sidi Ahmed would not be there. The house seems empty. Hm-m-m!"

BURKE TURNED to the door again, looked out, then slipped out into the hall and went to the stairs. A glance upward, and he ascended swiftly. The upstairs hall was before him dimly lighted by Moorish lanterns. From an open doorway down the corridor, a shaft of brighter light streamed across, and he approached softly.

"You fool!" came the voice of Madame Desaix. "It's more than any one else would pay!"

"Fifty thousand isn't enough," replied a man's voice, sullenly. Burke started. She was offering only fifty thousand! She meant to make money.

"Suppose I can get the offer increased, then?"

"Devil take you! Not a sou less than a quarter of a million, in cash!"

The woman was silent for a moment. Then, to the astonishment of Burke, she assented softly.

"Very well. If he'll pay that, when can we get the papers?"

"They are here; but you'll never find them!" The man burst into a mocking laugh that told of strong drink. "Sell them to Burke, yes, but no graft! Ten per cent and my debts paid—that's all you get. Oh, I know you! And you needn't look at me. The report isn't in my pockets; it's hidden, understand? Make him pay the price! I know Burke, the rascal knows what this report's worth. He'll pay!"

"Very well," she answered. "So it is hidden, is it? Then I'll make sure he will pay, and return with advance money. Get your precious document ready!"

The shaft of light was darkened by her figure. Burke had no escape. He pressed into the next doorway. The door yielded to his hand. He was in a dark and empty room, closing the door. He heard her pass by outside, and drew a breath of relief.

No time to waste! In three minutes she would find him gone from the salon. Before then, he must act.

Like a flash, he slipped out into the hall and went to the next room. He stepped in. Fronting him, seated at a table, was an officer in civilian clothes, the man whom Crepin had mentioned—Lieutenant Courtot. A young fellow, hard-eyed, hard-faced, wild surmise in his distended gaze, his features haggard and drawn by dissipation and recent drunkenness. So Courtot *was* the murderer!

Burke closed the door, stood with his back against it. A scheme leaped in his brain.

"You know me, Courtot! Not a word; it's life or death! They mean to kill us both—take the document from you, the money from me—understand? Can we get out of here unseen?"

Courtot leaped to his feet. Drunk he had been, but his brain was sharp enough.

"You know?" he exclaimed.

"Of course. I heard her talking with you. Can we get out of here? Quickly!"

"Yes, yes! The balcony—the gardens. Here!"

Courtot turned to the long windows and swung them open. An oath broke from him; he turned, darted back to the table, and caught up a heavy knotted stick such as Arabs use. Then he came out to the balcony, where Burke now stood.

Burke had no plan, beyond to get his man out of here and grab him. He swung himself over the rail, for the ground was not far below. He dropped, fell among flowers, and came lightly to his feet.

At this instant a sharp cry came from within the house. Courtot, half over the rail, paused there an instant, laughed harshly and let himself go. He came down heavily.

"Make for the gate!" exclaimed Burke.

"No, no!" Courtot, with a gasp of breath, came to his feet and caught at Burke's arm. "They have men there—"

"Nonsense! It's deserted!"

"Don't be a fool!" snapped Courtot. "They've been watching the gate and gardens. They wanted me to leave this way—I saw the men hiding! After I killed that rascal who—"

Burke turned on him. "Are you crazy?"

"I thought you knew! I had to pretend I was selling it. I killed that rascal Yusuf, poor Latrobe's orderly, and got it! Here, come along with me. Devil take it, my ankle's done for! There's a back gate. We may get out there—"

With a suppressed groan, Courtot started off, hobbling by aid of his stick.

No time for explanations! He followed Courtot, struck into a path and swung around the house. In front of them pealed a wild yell. A dark figure rushed at them. Burke struck at it savagely; it collapsed and was silent. The two went on. Then Courtot groaned, staggered, and plunged down. He scrambled up, standing on one leg.

"Leave me!" he gasped. "You can make it. My ankle—"

Another yell. Bushes and branches crashed. Burke turned, met with a furious onrush of figures. They were all around, everywhere! He heard Courtot cry out in agony, then something crashed against him.

BURKE'S THROBBING, hot brain awoke to his own name. "Monsieur Burke!"

"That you, Courtot?" he said faintly, and put out his hands. He could feel nothing. He was lying on a stone or tile floor. "Where are we?"

"I do not know. Listen! I have not long. They stabbed me— leave me alone, let me talk! You don't know about Latrobe after all? About his murder?"

Burke shivered in the darkness. "Not everything," he said. "Tell me."

"Upon the honor of a dying man!" gasped the other. "I have been in this house for three days, drunk, gambling, smoking. The Desaix woman and others—I am in their power, you comprehend? Blackmail. No escape. I am ruined, ruined!

"I was sober this morning. Yusuf was in the room next to mine. He had been smoking kief. It made him a madman! He came to himself, wanted to sell the document; he had stolen it for money. I heard them talking. What could I do? I am a disgraced man. Nobody would believe me. I went into his room this afternoon. He was smoking again. He thought I had come to arrest him and attacked me. Well, I was ready for him! I killed him and took the stick. It is hollow. It has the report hidden inside. Then I had to lie, pretend that I wanted to sell the document. That Desaix woman and Sidi Ahmed were here. They had me watched. If I tried to escape, they would kill me—and they have done it. The stick—"

His voice, becoming fainter and fainter, died away, bubbled, then was still.

Burke moved about. Presently he touched the body of Courtot. But there was no sign of the stick anywhere. The room was a small one.

After a time noises sounded at the door. Burke stretched out quickly, so that he could peep from between his nearly closed lids. The door creaked and swung open. Two Arabs stood there, one holding up a lantern. Burke did not know either of them.

"The devil! The officer is dead!" said one sharply. "We did not know he was hurt—a stab in the side, eh? This is bad. How about the other?"

"Unconscious," was the reply, as the lantern was lowered near Burke's face. "I'll tie him up. You run and tell madame about the officer."

One man departed. The other put down his lantern and brought cords from beneath his brown robe. He was bearded, squat, and powerful. He caught hold of Burke's right arm and reached for the left, then Burke had him, all unsuspecting. Burke seized him by the beard, dragged him forward off balance! The two grappled, went rolling across the floor.

They brought up against the wall. With a frantic effort, Burke flung himself around, came on top of the other. He still clung to the beard. The light of the lantern flashed on a knife, then the native's head was banged back against the floor! Relaxing, he lay stunned.

Burke stripped off the brown enveloping robe. Reaching for the cords, he bound the man, gagged him with the brass hilt of his knife tied between his jaws, and stood up. He slipped the ungainly robe over his head and drew up the hood, then took the lantern and shoved open the door. The key was still in the lock. He turned it, threw it away, and chuckled, then glanced quickly around.

A little summerhouse amid the gardens—and no escape! The beam of a flashlight struck full upon him. There was Madame Desaix, a dozen feet away, coming swiftly toward the door. Her voice lifted in Arabic.

"Fool! Bring out the dead man, quickly! We must get rid of the body before dawn!"

"It is already done!" Burke held up the lantern to hide his face from her. "By Allah, the man had bled to death!"

He saw now that she was alone, and his pulses leaped. Woman or not, he could not afford to hesitate! She was almost face to face with him now.

"And the other?" she demanded sharply. "The American? Where is he? We must shut his accursed mouth at once—"

"He is here," said Burke, and dropped his lantern. He caught her by the wrists, looked into her face. "Quiet, woman! Not a word out of you! Take me to the entrance and have your men open the gates."

For a moment she hung limp in his grasp.

"Ah!" she murmured. "You devil! Now I believe all they say about you! Very well. You have won. Will you promise to say no word?"

Burke's reaction gave her the chance she had sought. With a sudden terrific display of strength, she tore her hands free. Her nails clawed at his face, a scream burst from her, then she whipped out a tiny pistol.

"To me! Help!" she screamed. "He has tried to assault me—"

She fired point-blank, but excitement spoiled her aim. Cursing her ingenuity, Burke knocked up her pistol hand. She flung herself upon him bodily. She got her arms around him, fired again, trying to shoot him in the back, but failing. Shouts broke from the near-by house.

Desperate, Burke tripped her, wrenched away her arms. She caught at him, dragged him to the ground. He grappled with her frantically. Again she pulled the trigger.

This shot pierced her own throat.

Burke was no more than on his feet when they were upon him; not Arabs this time, but officers from the house. They stripped, away the robe; some of them recognized him.

"Murder! He has murdered her!" they cried out. "Here is his pistol. She is dead!"

Somebody, with a furious oath, lifted a weapon and brought it down. Struck for the second time over the head, Burke collapsed.

When he wakened, to cold daylight of early morning, he was in a prison cell, charged with the murder of Madame Desaix.

WHEN CREPIN entered the cell, Burke came to his feet. "You were long enough getting here! What's this absurd charge against me?"

"Unfortunately, it's not absurd," Crepin said, swinging a stick. "I heard you were here, and went direct to the Desaix villa. I've just come from there."

"Courtot! Did you find Courtot's body?"

Crepin's brows lifted. "What has that to do with it? His body was found early this morning on the other side of town. The poor devil was waylaid by Arabs, evidently."

Burke whistled slowly, appalled by what faced him.

"You have some explanation of all this?" said Crepin. "I know the pistol was her own, for it had her name on it. But she was heard to scream that she was being assaulted. You were found wearing an Arab robe, struggling with her. My friend, it looks bad!"

"You don't believe it!"

"No." Crepin shrugged. "I am waiting to hear your story. If you can explain all this, can make a convincing story of it, well enough!"

Explain! What he had to say was incredible. He realized it. He had not an atom of proof. Courtot's body had been taken care of. No one would believe his story unless—

Suddenly his gray eyes glowed.

"Come, Crepin! I am going to trust you," he exclaimed cheerfully. "Faith, if you were any other man on earth, I'd not take the chance! But I know you. The honor of an officer! You'll understand it. I'm going to tell you how and why poor Courtot died."

He related exactly what had taken place, all of it. Crepin listened with the keenest interest, only to shake his head when Burke had finished.

"Monsieur Burke, I believe you; no one else would!"

"Thanks to you, Crepin," exclaimed Burke, "every one will believe me!"

"I? Name of the devil! What do you mean?"

Burke nodded toward the stick in the hand of the intelligence officer.

"Where did you get it? If I'm not mistaken, that's Courtot's stick."

Crepin swore amazedly. "True! It was found in the garden. I was taking it with me to headquarters to—"

He seized the stick suddenly, held it across his knee, pulled violently. It flew into shreds. A tightly rolled clump of papers fell to the floor. Burke stooped, picked up the roll, and extended it with a smile.

"Latrobe's report, Captain Crepin."

The other seized it, looked at it, then caught Burke in his arms.

"I am glad! In half an hour you'll be out of this, my friend!"

"Thank you," returned Burke. "I trust you'll hurry, my dear Crepin. I have to arrange this afternoon about the delivery of some ammunition to the agent of the Berbers, and there's no time to lose. Our truce is ended, I think?"

"As soon as you are free, yes. Monsieur Burke, I salute you!"

Burke's laugh lightened the prison. The episode was ended.

VI

ENMITY

A dividend on hate!

SUNSET WAS at hand. The flags announcing evening prayer were up in the minarets of all the mosques. In Morocco, there are no muezzins.

Denis Burke left his car behind the hotel, passed through the lobby, and strode out across the terraces and down the garden walk. He meant to spend half an hour, as he usually did upon coming to Meknez, with this incomparable sunset view. Here, the Transatlantique, the great new hotel, stood on a height like an outpost of the modern French city. Across the wide ravine of the Bou Fekrane, rose the ancient Arab city, with its miles of enormous, massive walls.

Suddenly Burke saw her, and paused. At sight of this woman any one must have paused, much less a romantic Irishman.

As she stood in the sunset light the breeze whipped her garments about the outlines of her body. Her profile was like that of a fine cameo. She must have arrived this afternoon, for no such person had been around the hotel at noon. Then he recalled that the weekly boat from France had reached Casablanca last night. She must have come on to Meknez by the day train.

To his surprise, she turned and saw him there, then approached with a smile.

"So you have put the message through for me?" she began, then checked herself in confusion. Her face changed. "Oh, your pardon; the sunlight dazzled me. I thought you were the hotel manager. You see, he has been trying to reach my brother, Captain Arcachon, at the aviation camp. I—the error—"

Burke bowed, but an icy hand gripped him.

"Arcachon? Not Captain Raoul Arcachon?" he said in a low voice, before he thought. Her eyes widened.

"Oh! Then you know him? You see, I got here only an hour ago. He failed to meet my boat at Casablanca last night. I came on by train to-day."

Burke glanced about for some way out; there was none. He must go through with it now. She had read the look in his face, and advanced swiftly to him, her lips half parted, her hand extended in appeal.

"What is it? What is wrong?"

Burke gathered himself for the ordeal.

"I'm a poor hand at breaking bad news—" he began. She straightened a little. Her deep blue eyes were level, unafraid.

"I understand. A crash?"

"Three days ago. It was over at Volubilis, the Roman city. I happened to be there, and saw it myself. You have friends, relatives?"

She shook her head, and gently removed her hand from his clasp.

"No. He and I—alone. I—I think I'll sit down. Please don't leave me. Then he is dead?"

Burke inclined his head. His bronzed features had lost their usual touch of reckless laughter. He led her to a table on the terrace. Beckoning a waiter, he ordered two brandies; he needed one himself, after this. Yet she took it bravely enough.

About them rose the voices of tourists from the other tables. Around the steps below loafed a group of hotel guides, in their raiment of gorgeous hues. The hotel was built along the hill crest; the rooms in the low wings opened directly on the gardens. Each room had a little balcony; thus, to gain any of these rooms, one did not have to pass through the hotel, but might merely step over the balcony rail.

Watching the woman, Denis Burke thought he had never seen so delicate a beauty as hers. He placed one of his cards before her.

"Permit me; I am not a tourist, but I live here in Morocco. To be of any assistance to you would greatly honor me."

She glanced at the card, then lifted her eyes.

"Thank you, Monsieur Burke. You say that you saw it happen? And you are certain that he is dead? Ah!" Astonished, Burke could have sworn that this exclamation held untold relief. She took up the tiny glass of cognac and drained it.

"I regret being the bearer of such news," Burke said gently. "Your grief—"

She met his eyes with a smile.

"Grief? Well, at least it is a shock," she said, quite composedly. "Regret? No, no! I must make you understand. You are a gentleman; I may dare to ask you for advice. You must comprehend that I had small love for this brother, small grief for him. Raoul was older than I; he was harsh, stern, and believed that he knew what was best for me. The family money was in his hands. He was the head of the family, you see. Well, he forced me to come here."

Burke listened to all this in the utmost astonishment. For a moment she glanced away, then her gaze came back to him. She nodded, as with decision.

"Yes, I shall ask you for help, since you have offered it," she went on. "I was brought here to marry a man whom I detest with all my heart. Now that Raoul is dead, I am free; I need obey no one. But I know this man, and I am afraid of him. Is it too much if I ask that you, an entire stranger, protect me from him?"

Burke's pulses leaped. He knew what it meant to interfere in the domestic policy of a French family; but this was different. As she had said, she was now free.

"With all my heart!" he exclaimed blithely, and his heart showed in his eyes. "And who is the man?"

"Captain de Nemours, of the aviation corps."

Burke fairly beamed.

"Good! The best news I've heard in a long time!" he cried. "I know Nemours, and he knows me to his cost. We're anything but friends. Yes, a thousand times yes; I shall be honored to be of service!"

"It is kind of you." She extended her hand across the table, a shadowy smile just touching her lips. "Thank you, my friend. I think I shall go to my room; I have many things to do. To-morrow, perhaps?"

"If you'll lunch with me. Here at the hotel, shall we say?"

"Gladly."

BURKE WENT back to his car, and drove to the little French hotel he frequented in Meknez; a small hotel, in the new city. As he drove, his eyes glistened. They would lunch together on the morrow, eh? And Nemours—that was the best of all.

That evening he went to the house of Caid es Salem, in the old Arab city. Here were the caid and his eldest son; a laughing, wealthy Arab merchant from Fez; an Algerian, a private banker; and Souzan, manager of the local bank. It was a sedately riotous evening.

On behalf of these others, Burke had neatly outwitted a French exploitation company, which had grabbed some rich lands belonging to the caid. When he fought with rascals, Burke was not always polite. The guiding but invisible hand behind this land grab had been that of Nemours. The aviation officer was making his fortune in Morocco.

If Burke had friends in this land, he also had enemies, as needs must a man who lives by his wits. He had several times run into Nemours; a brutal man, whose money and army position had enabled him to turn some pretty deals—and some not so pretty. Nemours was not particular.

So, although Burke did not mention meeting the girl to these friends of his, there was some little talk of Captain de Nemours. The dark, alert Souzan, turned to Burke.

"I hear," he said, "that our friend Nemours is intimate with El Hajib, lord of the Zerghou Berbers and a very rich man. It is rumored that Nemours has a hand in supplying the army with sheep, most of which come from the Berbers."

"So? This El Hajib was in the city to-day," spoke up Caid es Salem, stroking his gray beard. "It is the first time in months that he has left his hill castle. Beware of Berber knives, Sidi Burke! This man Nemours is a bad enemy."

"Bah!" Burke laughed. "My wits are sharp, and your spies are sharper; if there's any danger, you'll hear of it."

"May Allah avert the evil omen of your words!" the caid exclaimed.

"Faith, luck is what you make it; and I'm not done with that chap yet." With a laugh, Burke rose. "Well, I'm off. Talk all night if you like, and peace be with you."

"And with you, peace," was the response.

That night, Burke dreamed of golden hair, and it was a pleasant dream.

The luncheon engagement was pleasant, also. Before their meal was well begun, he learned that her name was Isabel. Some ten minutes later, an Arab attendant brought her a card. She glanced at it, then looked up at Burke, agitation in her eyes.

"It is he, Nemours! I cannot see him. Will you please send him away? Tell him the truth; get rid of him."

"Will I, indeed?"

Burke hummed a gay air as he strode out into the gorgeous reception room of the hotel. Nemours was there, handsome in the midnight-blue and gold of the aviation corps. He eyed Burke inquiringly as the latter approached.

"My dear fellow," Burke drawled, "I'm happy to tell you that you have no business whatever here. Isabel doesn't marry you at all. She doesn't want even to see you."

Nemours shrugged, but his dark gaze narrowed with anger.

"So you've intervened in this affair, Monsieur Burke? Very well. *Au revoir.*"

He turned and walked off, a compact, powerful figure of a man. Burke glanced after him, then rubbed his chin thoughtfully. This was odd. He had not expected the Frenchman to take it in this manner, without so much as an oath.

Then, all of a sudden, without any warning, things happened. One of the hotel guides came to him as he stood there. He was a slim brown youth who spoke softly in Arabic.

"Sidi, I am the brother's son of Caid es Salem."

"May Allah favor him and you." Burke's gray eyes leaped alert. "Well? What is it?"

"A message to give you. A year ago, El Hajib obtained his fourth wife; she came from France, by the help of Captain de

Nemours. Now he has divorced her, because she displeases him. Yesterday, El Hajib came to Meknez. With him came the divorced wife. Her name is Victoire. You talked with her on the terrace last evening. To-day you are eating with her. That is all."

BURKE SWALLOWED hard; for a moment he stood motionless, a flame in his eyes. Not for an instant did he doubt the truth of this message; but it might be some mistake. Then he strode into the lobby and crossed to the desk.

He snatched up the telephone and called the bank. By good luck, he caught Souzan there.

"Burke speaking, at the Transatlantique; important. Call me back in five minutes, like a good chap. Tell me whether a woman named Arcachon was aboard the boat arriving night before last at Casablanca."

Souzan assented. Burke lighted a cigarette and waited. Within three minutes came the return call.

"I have the passenger list here. No such name appears, nor was there any woman traveling alone."

"That settles it. Allah bless you!"

Souzan, who believed neither in Allah nor any other deity, grunted scornfully.

Although he gave no outward sign of it, Burke returned to the luncheon table with his brain in turmoil. It was not strange that Caid es Salem should warn him. For long centuries, Berber heads have been piled by the hundreds in every Arab town of Morocco; for centuries the two races have cherished a bitter and bloody hatred.

Burke shivered slightly; how completely she had hooked him! Then he sat down, met her inquiring gaze, and broke into his carefree laugh.

"He's gone. He'll trouble you no more, upon my word."

She thanked him beautifully. What an actress, he thought; what a lovely creature! Inwardly, of course, she was nothing of the sort.

Burke knew what she must be, what any woman must be, who would leave France for such a bridal in Africa. Nemours had managed all that for El Hajib, then. And her whole story about Captain Arcachon had been a lie. She had been carefully planted to meet Burke, gain his sympathy, make friends. Nemours had figured the whole thing out, and had come here to-day merely to play his own role. To what end?

"Well, my dear," Burke said cheerfully, "and what shall we do this afternoon? I'm at your service, and so is my car."

She would like to drive; Morocco was all new to her. Burke did not even smile at this response. Sooner or later she would spring the trap.

For two hours, Burke drove her about Meknez. He showed her the miles of enormous walls the great Mulai Ismail had built; he showed her the palace of Ismail's English sultana, the new French city, the aviation field where her supposed brother had worked. When they came back to the hotel, he gave her his warm, quick smile.

"Should you like a native dinner to-night? I have friends in the Arab town, yonder; it might be a new experience."

"Oh, gladly!" she exclaimed, but he saw her eyes flicker slightly. "And, my friend, there is something else. I started to ask it yesterday, but hesitated. To-night there is a moon. Could you take me to the place where Raoul died. The Roman city?"

"Volubilis and moonlight—oh, romance!" Burke cried blithely. "By all odds a historic spot, both for Morocco and for you. I'm glad you didn't love that brother of yours."

"So am I." She smiled. "Au revoir, then. Let us plan on reaching Volubilis about ten, when the moon will be high."

Burke assented, but when he drove away, he chuckled to himself. So the trap was to be sprung that night. And how had she known about the moon? From Nemours, of course. Ten o'clock. Bah! A rather stupid trap, after all.

From his own hotel, Burke telephoned Caid es Salem, asking if he might bring the divorced wife of El Hajib to dinner that evening, and depart early. The old caid assented with a laugh. The Arabs and the Chinese have one thing in common. Their humor is rooted in cruelty.

ISABEL, ALIAS Victoire, was a finished actress. To watch her, one would think that never before had she dipped that lovely hand in a great brazen kettle, dismembering a chicken or a leg of lamb. With the couscous it was very different, however. When it came to kneading the little ball of rice and slipping it into the mouth, native style, she forgot herself once or twice and did it neatly. And Caid es Salem grinned.

They departed early. They said farewell and started for Volubilis, with the moon behind horizon clouds. Then Isabel, learning they would reach the Roman ruins at nine instead of ten, was distinctly dismayed.

Poor Arcachon had crashed at the very edge of the excavations, far on the west side; Burke knew the exact spot. To reach it, he must take a certain path that led through the deep ravine bordering the Roman ruins. He had no intention of visiting that spot, though. He had ideas of his own.

They drove almost in silence until, when they came into the great sweep of curving road, Burke pointed to a faint cluster of lights far above, and the dim mass of a town vaguely white in the moonlight.

"Mulai Idris; the second most holy shrine of the Moslem world. The tomb of Idris, whose descendants have ruled this land for a thousand years. Two pilgrimages to this place, in Moslem eyes, equal the great pilgrimage to Mecca. Does history bore you, madame?"

She caught her breath slightly. "No. But why do you call me madame?"

"Ah, to-night I might call you anything!" Burke's laugh rang out. "What are names? We're about to walk streets where a British legion once trod the stones, about to stand in a Roman forum. It was there the wild tribes later took Idris for leader, founding this whole empire. Look up at his tomb. No Christians are allowed there at night, even now. Doesn't that thrill you?"

"No. But you might," she said softly, leaning against him a little. He laughed again.

"Good! Very soon, I promise you a thrill. Here we are, and the moon expected us."

The moon, indeed, had quite emerged from the clouds. They turned from the highway into the short, rough road leading to the museum and buildings; all deserted and dark. Burke halted the car, helped Isabel out, and guided her past the buildings to the path that ran across the wide ravine.

The moonlight flooded down in silver glory. Here was utter isolation, the stark majesty of a dead and disinterred city, in part restored to life. Columns, walls, and arches stretched on all sides. Burke turned to his companion, with an exultant word.

"Victoria! Victoria!"

"What?" She halted. One hand went to her heart. "What do you mean?"

"A Roman word, my dear!" said Burke lightly. "Perhaps you recall it from past incarnations. A little farther on, if you please. Look at this great block of stone! I've a fancy to see you standing on it, in the moonlight. It was the rostrum of the forum, they say. Will you oblige me?"

She pressed his arm against her side, as they walked on. Then he aided her to mount the great block of stone. Her cloak fell away. Burke caught it, drew it clear of her.

The moonlight glinted from her hair in soft radiance. The breeze draped the thin silken dress about her body in splendid flowing lines. She lifted her arms, lifted her head, stood there in incredible loveliness. Burke, impressionable Irishman that he was, thrilled to the sight.

"Your foot a little forward—ah, glorious! You're sheer enchantment, my dear. I wanted to see you just this once, so. I didn't dream you'd be so lovely. You know the 'Winged Victory'?

You are that statue, brought to life, made flesh, but a hundred times more beautiful. You're the most splendid thing I ever saw."

She was smiling. Burke held up his hand to her.

"Well, it's over, so come along. My dear, you've given me a memory of ineffable beauty, a gift that covers a multitude of sins. Come, Victoire."

She had stepped down, when the word struck her. She turned, her lips parted, trembling. She stared at him, then spoke.

"Victoire! What do you mean by that?"

Burke shrugged.

"This is a savage country, but don't be afraid. I don't fight women. I suppose that even El Hajib was sensible of your beauty?"

Her smile had frozen. Now it slowly died out. A dreadful silence fell.

A CHANGE crept over her. Comprehension widened her eyes, a growing terror quivered in her face. She was leaning forward now, her fingers blindly plucking at her dress. Burke threw the cloak about her shoulders, but she paid no heed.

"Then—you know!"

At his nod, she fell back against the stone block, sobbing softly in the moonlight. Burke turned away and lighted a cigarette, and gazed up at the star-shaped city of Mulai Idris, a white splotch on its dark hill.

After a little he turned again. Now she was leaning wearily against the stone. Her face was lined and drawn.

"What do you mean to do?" she asked in a dead voice.

"Take you home and say good night," Burke responded. "You've failed."

"You—you don't understand," she broke out, her fingers twisting about one another. "I had no choice. It was my chance to go back. *Mon Dieu!* I have been in agony, for you are a good man. But it was too late. Twenty thousand francs—"

"Eh?" Burke started slightly. "As much as that? And when were you to get it?"

"To-night. Nemours was coming to the hotel to give me the money."

"After they killed me in the ravine, eh?"

"No, no!" She burst into passionate speech. "At first, I did not care; it made no difference what they did. But after meeting you, I saw Nemours and refused. Then he explained that you were not to be hurt. It was only a matter of money, of making your friends ransom you. Nothing else. I swear it! You must believe me!"

"Very well, I believe you," Burke assured her, though he believed nothing of the sort. "Is Nemours a friend of yours?"

She shivered. "A friend?" A bitter laugh came from her. "I came to Morocco, thinking he and I were to be married. Instead, he sold me. El Hajib paid him a huge sum. You cannot realize what it meant; I was helpless. And now this chance to get back to France, to fold back all that chapter of my life as though it had not existed. What did I care? But he promised not to harm you."

"Then El Hajib was merely to carry me off?"

"Yes. I was to return to Meknez. Nemours comes to my room at eleven, to pay me; he comes from the outside, by the balcony."

Burke glanced at his watch.

"I see. Well, come along, my dear. The show's over; we'll get away before El Hajib arrives, and leave him waiting for me. Wrap that cloak tightly; it's a bit chilly."

They went away in silence, gained the car, encountered no one.

It was a few minutes past eleven when Nemours appeared at the rail of the balcony, outside the room occupied by Isabel. He was in uniform. If anything went wrong, this gave him entire protection. An officer, in Morocco, can get away with anything.

An instant he paused at the rail, there in the moonlight. Then he stepped over it. The room door was ajar, the room inside all dark. He stepped across the balcony and pushed open the door.

"Victoire!" he called softly. "Are you back? Is everything all right?"

"Quite all right," said Burke.

Nemours was knocked backward with terrific force. He fell on the floor of the balcony. He half came to his feet, and was knocked back again. This time, he stirred for a moment, then lay quiet.

Burke stood over him, cursing softly and sucking his knuckles. Then he knelt and went through the man's pockets. After a little he picked up the limp form, rose, and with an effort carried Nemours to the balcony rail. He dropped the man's figure over into a clump of flowers, and tossed the gold-laced képi after it.

Coming back into the room, he switched on the light. The figure of the woman stood pressed against the wall, staring, her face deadly pale. Burke tossed a sheaf of thousand-franc notes on the table.

"There you are. Rout out the hotel manager now, this moment. Have him hire a car for you, and you'll reach Casablanca tonight. The boat for Marseille leaves at eight in the morning. Once off, he can't stop you. Better luck attend you in future."

He lifted her hand, touched his lips to it, then was gone.

SOME MONTHS later, Burke received a packet from Paris by mail. He opened it in some surprise, and from it took a small gilded replica of the "Winged Victory." But, from this replica, each wing had been carefully broken. No name, no card, was inclosed.

Burke understood. He placed it on his desk, regarded it with smiling eyes, and blew it a kiss.

"The 'Wingless Victory,' eh? So things are all going well with you," he murmured. "Thanks, my dear. The account is closed."

ABOUT THE AUTHOR

H. BEDFORD-JONES is a Canadian by birth, but not by profession, having removed to the United States at the age of one year. For over twenty years he has been more or less profitably engaged in writing and traveling. As he has seldom resided in one place longer than a year or so and is a person of retiring habits, he is somewhat a man of mystery; more than once he has suffered from unscrupulous gentlemen who impersonated him—one of whom murdered a wife and was subsequently shot by the police, luckily after losing his alias.

The real Bedford-Jones is an elderly man, whose gray hair and precise attire give him rather the appearance of a retired foreign diplomat. His hobby is stamp collecting, and his collection of Japan is said to be one of the finest in existence. At present writing he is en route to Morocco, and when this appears in print he will probably be somewhere on the Mojave Desert in company with Erle Stanley Gardner.

Questioned as to the main facts in his life, he declared there was only one main fact, but it was not for publication; that his life had been uneventful except for numerous financial losses, and that his only adventures lay in evading adventurers. In his younger years he was something of an athlete, but the encroachments of age preclude any active pursuits except that of motoring. He is usually to be found poring over his stamps, working at his typewriter, or laboring in his California rose garden, which is one of the sights of Cathedral Cañon, near Palm Springs.

www.ingramcontent.com/pod-product-compliance
Lightning Source LLC
Chambersburg PA
CBHW070940250626
47159CB00009B/3325